Claude Filion was born and raised in Ontario and is a graduate of York University, Cambridge University, and McGill University. He has been a lawyer since 1986. He has been a public speaker since 1998. He loves animals, and is devoted to the dogs and birds who share his home. He also enjoys reading, writing, walking his dogs, and playing tennis and pickleball.

To Tommy, Bobby and Daisy.

To Kim

Thank you for your purchase.
Enjoy the novel. Nice to meet
you. Enjoy,

Claude Filion

# A Dog's Last Wish

A Tale of Companionship

Austin Macauley Publishers™
London • Cambridge • New York • Sharjah

**Ordering Information**
Quantity sales: Special discounts are available on quantity purchases by corporations, associations, and others. For details, contact the publisher at the address below.

**Publisher's Cataloging-in-Publication data**
Filion, Claude
A Dog's Last Wish

ISBN 9798891555181 (Paperback)
ISBN 9798891555198 (ePub e-book)

Library of Congress Control Number: 2024902084

www.austinmacauley.com/us

First Published 2024
Austin Macauley Publishers LLC
40 Wall Street, 33rd Floor, Suite 3302
New York, NY 10005
USA

mail-usa@austinmacauley.com
+1 (646) 5125767

I wish to express my gratitude for the excellent services rendered to Tommy, Bobby, and Daisy, by Mary Lynn Lackie, DVM, and Elizabeth Motluk, DVM, (Village Veterinary Clinic); Nicole Lalande (Eastway Pet Resort); Lynn Menard (Everything Raw Doggie Café); Chloé Bissonnette (Aux Pitous Adorables); Madison Peterman (Groomer Madison); and John Philip Stratton (John Philip Photography).

I also wish to express my gratitude the editing services rendered by Adam Paul (Fiverr), and Julie Wehbe (Julie Wehbe Online Services LTD).

# Chapter 1

After work one day, I left the office and drove home – a small apartment that I shared with my two dogs, Tommy and Bobby. As soon as I opened the door, Bobby scampered to greet me. I heard a shuffling noise, turned, and to my horror, saw Tommy lying on the floor, stuck under a desk. Made of steel, it had a writing platform and a base, joined by two vertical rails about eight inches apart. He had walked backward, wedged his hips between the rails, and pushed himself through them until he could push no further.

Barely conscious and breathing slowly, Tommy made no effort to greet me. There were signs of a struggle. A few pens had fallen from the desk, tufts of hair were spread around him, and his face was swollen. He seemed a forlorn creature.

I pressed my fingers gently over his limbs and joints, but felt no broken bones. Watching for signs of discomfort, I slid his body past the rails and laid him on the floor. After a few seconds, I lifted him, but he was unsteady on his feet, so I put him back on his side before he could lose his balance.

I went to see my neighbor who rented an apartment on the same floor. As soon as he answered the door, he saw that I was distraught, and asked, "What's wrong?"

"Tommy is hurt," I said. "I must take him to the animal clinic. Can you help me move him to the car?"

"Yes, of course."

He followed me to my apartment. We unfolded a blanket, laid Tommy on top of it, lifted him, and walked to my car, parked in front of the building. As we walked down the hall, we met another neighbor who agreed to keep an eye on Bobby in my absence.

I opened the rear passenger door, and we put Tommy on the floor. The car had no back seat, so he had plenty of room to stretch his legs. After thanking my neighbor, I drove away.

Tommy was my yellow Labrador Retriever. He weighed seventy lbs., and had a large head, a strong neck, a stocky build, short limbs, and a thick tail. He was a handsome dog with wide brown eyes. A natural shadow complemented the color of his eyes, making them appear larger. All his life, he received attention for his good looks. His coat was light yellow, giving him a youthful look, even in old age, when arthritis was crippling his limbs.

He was calm around people, especially children. His favorite occasion was Halloween night. He sat in the front yard, dazzled by the sights and sounds of children laughing in their masks and costumes. They cooed and petted him, but sometimes, tripped over their costumes, and fell on top of him. To avoid contact, he shifted his weight from one side to the other but never retaliated. He was also calm around animals, except dogs who challenged him to fight.

Although he never instigated a fight, he never ran from one either. Regardless of the other dog's size, he fought until it withdrew. On my way to the clinic, I recalled two other incidents in which Tommy had gotten himself in trouble. Once, I had left him alone in the car to run an errand. When I returned to the car, I saw him frantically trying to free one of his legs from a trap door in the seat. I pushed the trap door open and freed his leg. Although he limped a little, he soon recovered. On another occasion, I had left Tommy at my brother's house. In the backyard, there was a gazebo covered with netting. Tommy's collar became entangled in the netting, and he began to spin around his collar, causing it to squeeze tightly around his neck. My sister-in-law heard his squeals and untangled the collar.

But today's incident was more ominous. Tommy was much older now, and I suspected that he had been stuck under the desk for hours. Fearful that his life might be slipping away, I turned around to look. To my relief, he seemed to be resting comfortably. As I drove, I reached back with my arm and patted him on the shoulder.

I asked myself whether his injury was so serious that he should be euthanized. Tommy was old, ailing, and disabled. When would be the right time to put him down? I asked friends for advice, but they politely deflected the question. Gradually, I came to believe that I should keep him alive as long as he had a strong appetite for food. All his life, he loved food. He always knew when it was time to eat, and never hesitated to remind me if I had forgotten. He watched me prepare his meal and devoured it as if it were his last. When he was done, he licked the bowl clean and fell asleep. Frankly, I would have preferred to see him take smaller bites, and chew them purposefully, but he gobbled them whole.

I kept second-guessing myself. Was I prolonging his suffering?

Was I putting too much emphasis on his appetite?

# Chapter 2

I parked my car at the back of the clinic. A technician met me, lifted Tommy in her arms, and carried him inside. In the past, Tommy had enjoyed being at the clinic. He sniffed the reception counter, stood on the weight scale, greeted other dogs, and observed the cats in an adjoining room. When he saw the veterinarian, he wagged his tail, and eagerly followed her to the examination room. He remained still as she felt his body, listened to his heart, took his temperature, and stuck needles in him. He panted when she spoke to him.

But today, he was unresponsive. She pressed her fingers softly over his body and confirmed that nothing was broken. After a brief examination, she noted that he was dehydrated. I was shocked. The reason for his last visit to the clinic had been dehydration. To prevent a recurrence, I mixed his food with water. I knew he was drinking enough water, but he seemed to be expelling it just as quickly.

The veterinarian also commented on Tommy's demeanor. He was passive and withdrawn. "Is he this lethargic at home?" she asked.

I shook my head, and said, "No. At home, he's quite alert. And he loves to eat. As long as he enjoys his food, I think I should keep him alive." I paused and thought of an analogy. *Suppose Tommy lived in a flimsy shack, and asked me to help him. Instead, I came along with a bulldozer and razed his shack to the ground. He would be sorry he had asked me for help.*

"Tommy might be in poor health, but he still wants to live, and he's asking me to help him feel better, not put him down."

"Euthanasia is final and irreversible," she said. "You have to be sure. You'll know when it's time. I suggest you leave him here overnight. We'll hydrate him. By tomorrow, he should be strong enough to go home." She hesitated. "Of course, you understand that he'll be alone in the clinic after it closes tonight." She was implying that he might die alone.

"I understand," I said, kissing Tommy on the forehead.

On the next day, I spoke to the veterinarian who told me that Tommy was fully hydrated, and anxious to go home. When I met her at the clinic, she showed me x-rays taken the night before. A few of the vertebrae in his spine had fused. There was a stain on his gall bladder. She suspected cancer. She informed me of other issues but confirmed that he was well enough to go home, and instructed me to keep a close eye on him. I promised to call her if his condition deteriorated.

After thanking the veterinarian, I clasped Tommy around the belly and eased him forward. With the support I gave him, he was able to move slowly. A technician helped me lay him down in the car. In a soft voice, she bade him farewell. I drove away.

Tommy was a seasoned passenger. On average, he had spent an hour a day in the car, shuttling between home and the daycare kennel, without ever showing signs of discomfort. But this time, he began to whimper as soon as we left the clinic. I sang him his favorite tunes, hoping to distract him. One was David Bowie's "Space Oddity," a song about Major Tom, an astronaut lost in space. Another was "Danny Boy," the famous Irish ballad about a father longing for his son.

In the past, he had enjoyed hearing the melodies, but today, he whined and shifted. I stopped the car on the side of the road, praised him, then resumed the drive home. He became more fidgety. I considered returning to the clinic, but by then, it had closed for the night. "You'll be fine once we get home," I assured him, trying to assure myself. I opened all the windows. Outside air rushed inside the car, distracting him. He stopped whining.

When we arrived home, I lifted him out of the car and led him inside the building. One of the residents opened the front door for us. Bobby met us at the door of my apartment.

After dinner, I took Bobby for a walk in the neighborhood. Near the end of the walk, I began to feel unwell. I felt pain radiating from my left arm to my fingers, and from my chest to my jaw. I started to perspire. I was short of breath and felt dizzy and nauseous. I stopped to rest on a bench, then labored at home, where I tried to read a book, but the pain worsened.

Was I having a heart attack? People I knew had been sidelined by one, and my best friend had succumbed to one. Was it my turn? I got into a panic. Would I survive? Would

I be hospitalized? Who would replace me at the office? Who would pay my bills? Who would take care of my dogs?

The answers to these questions would have to wait. Before long, I was asleep.

# Chapter 3

After a delay I can't measure, I awoke in the middle of nowhere. I knew I was outside. The air was cool, the ground was wet, and a dense fog smothered me, emitting an earthy odor. I turned one way then another, hoping to recognize something, anything, that would help me find my bearings, but the fog was too jealous to reveal any hint.

I heard dogs barking, birds chirping, insects droning, and steel wheels grinding along railroad tracks. I wondered what was behind this shroud. Then, I walked through a boulder, the size of a small car.

Puzzled, I turned around and tried to kick the boulder, but my foot sliced through it, causing me to stumble.

Little by little, the fog grew thinner. I saw shadows, then shapes and colors. I detected the faint outline of shrubs, leaves, branches, and tree trunks. Eventually, the fog lifted, and I saw a large park all around me. One side was bounded by a layer of trees, mainly maples, birches, and pines. The other side was bounded by railway tracks. At one end, there was a skating arena, and at the other end, a swimming pool. In the middle, there were tennis courts, play structures, and a boulder.

I felt none of the pain and nausea from the night before and took a deep, deep breath to savor the moment. Young and invigorated, I decided to test my fitness. I sprinted from one end of the park to the other and stopped at the top of a slope peppered with trees. As I ran down the slope, I weaved around the trees in my path, as if they were poles on a slalom course. At the bottom of the slope, I glanced at the arena in front of me. It was a rectangular structure made of concrete blocks, and covered by a dome of corrugated metal. Next to the arena, there were railroad tracks. I ran along the tracks, passed the play structures, made a right turn at the swimming pool, then headed up a slope to the boulder. By then, I had been sprinting for a few minutes, yet my pulse and breathing were normal. I ran along the same course again and completed it in less time. No matter how fast I ran, I felt I could run faster, and no matter how long I ran, I felt I could run longer.

I heard barking in the distance and saw two dogs running toward me. Recognizing my own Tommy and Bobby, I smiled, waved both arms, and called their names. When the dogs were close, I kneeled and opened my arms. Tails wagging, they jumped on me, and knocked me over. They hovered over me, tagged me with their noses, and licked my face.

Tommy saw a tennis ball on the ground, and grabbed it with his teeth. Standing in front of me, he grunted, pulled his ears back, wagged his tail, and flashed the ball at me. I tried to take it from him, but he trotted away. I followed him, and caught up to him. He dropped the ball, barked, ran around me, and then started to jump up and down. Meantime, Bobby stood over the ball, and stared at it, until

I took it, and threw it over his head. It bounced once on the ground, and he jumped to catch it in mid-air.

“Hey, follow me,” I yelled, sprinting away from them. The dogs ran after me, and quickly gained on me. As they overtook me, I swerved, and ran in another direction. When they noticed, they turned my way, and as they approached, I swerved again. We repeated this pattern for several minutes. When we finally stopped, we were still breathing normally. None of us were winded.

I sat on the ground, and watched the dogs wrestle playfully. Bobby was my chocolate Labrador Retriever. Seven years old, he was taller than Tommy. His head was narrow, and his neck and tail were thin. He had a long muzzle. The dark color of his coat highlighted his white hair, which had been visible from an early age.

He spent weekdays at a daycare kennel. His favorite pastime was to collect toys in the yard and guard them from other dogs, whom he considered to be looters. He was an incorrigible retriever of all things. When he wanted to fetch, he found a ball and stared at it until someone took his hint, picked up the ball, and threw it. He and I sometimes played fetch at the kennel. He never stopped to rest, even in the sweltering heat. He was prepared to fetch anywhere, anytime, even inside the apartment. When I lobbed a ball over his head, he scampered after it on the laminate floor. The floor was slippery, which added to his fun.

He was competitive and driven. When the staff at the kennel threw a ball, he was the first dog to fetch it. Frustrated, one dog retaliated by nipping him on the leg. To prevent injury, the staff decided to isolate him from the pack and play with him alone.

Bobby was very possessive. He seemed to think that the streets and sidewalks in the neighborhood belonged to him. When he met trespassers, he barked and lunged aggressively. I looked around me constantly to avoid other pedestrians.

Both dogs loved to walk. They insisted on walking every day, regardless of weather conditions. Whereas Tommy walked beside me, and when he was older behind me, Bobby walked in front of us. He pulled so hard that I had to get rid of his neck collar and fit him with a breast collar which put pressure on his chest, instead of his throat.

Tommy and Bobby loved each other dearly. They snuggled and kissed, and slept next to each other. They wrestled but never fought. Bobby was the leader. From the very first day, he led on walks. He also insisted on being the first to eat, the first to drink, the first to step through a doorway, and the first to receive affection. Nevertheless, he revered Tommy, and stuck to him like glue, especially when we went hiking in unfamiliar places.

I stood up and started to reflect. A few hours earlier, I had been an old man, barely able to run a few steps without stopping to catch my breath. I walked regularly, but slowly, and the walks caused my legs to ache. Yet, in this park, I felt as fit as a fiddle.

Tommy was an even bigger surprise. He had crippling arthritis. His loss of mobility had been gradual. I first noticed it when he started to limp, and trail Bobby and me on walks. His limbs were stiff, and he seemed to be walking on stilts. As time went on, he lagged further and further behind and stopped to rest more often.

Eventually, I had to walk the dogs separately. Every night, after dinner, Bobby and I went around the neighborhood. Afterward, Tommy and I went around the block.

Once, Tommy met a cat in a neighbor's driveway. As usual, he barked and charged, or should I say hobbled, but the cat just looked the other way. When Tommy tried to tag it with his nose, the cat struck it with its paw. Tommy turned to me in shock. "Poor Tommy," I said, smiling. "Your days of bullying cats are behind you."

Near the end, he showed no interest in the local sights and sounds, as if walking sapped all of his attention.

One night, he refused to walk at all. When we left the apartment building, he stepped off the ramp, picked a spot on the front lawn, circled his spot a few times, and sat down. I sat beside him, petted him, and talked to him, as he watched the hustle and bustle of the street. When he was ready, Tommy got up, relieved himself on the lawn, and then hobbled up the ramp to the front entrance.

Every night, we sat on that spot. If it rained, we sat under the roof of the front entrance. People and dogs, many of whom had crossed paths with him over the years, stopped to greet him and show him affection. When asked how Tommy was feeling, I replied that he was stable and comfortable.

One night, to my surprise, he walked past his spot, and stopped on the sidewalk, waiting for me to lead him across the street. He hobbled and limped around the block until we came to a corner, where he started to rock back and forth. For the first time, I realized that there was a slope on the street, so slight it was barely visible, but so steep it stopped him in his tracks. I placed my hands under his belly and eased him forward. The added support enabled him to move forward.

This was his last walk. From then on, we sat on the front lawn and only took a few steps when Tommy wanted to relieve himself.

In his lifetime, he and I had walked more than five thousand hours together. We walked along streets, sidewalks, trails, forests, and mountains. We walked in good, bad, hot, freezing, dry, and wet conditions. He chased cats, rabbits, squirrels, raccoons, deer, and other dogs.

Near the end, Tommy became too weak to move under his own power. I tried various devices to support him. I put Bobby's breast collar on him, but he slipped out of it. I sat him in a utility cart used to haul heavy objects, but he squirmed off it. Then, I bought a leather strap designed to carry fire logs. Wrapping it around his belly, I held him up and eased him forward. The strap worked well, but he leaned heavily on it, and I began to suspect that the pressure would bruise his ribs. So, I clasped my hands under his belly and eased him forward. To remove the stress of his weight on my back, I rested my elbows on my knees.

Finally, one day, my neighbor and I found a last resort to move him. We laid him on a blanket and carried him to the car.

Early one morning, I was awakened by the sound of pitter-patter in the apartment and rose to see Tommy walking backward in circles as if he were chasing his tail in reverse.

His heart was strong, but his limbs were weak. Near the end, he had so little mobility that he urinated on himself while lying on the front lawn, and waited for me to wipe him clean with a wet cloth. When we went inside, my eyes welled with tears. The end was coming soon, all too soon.

The outside temperature was dropping. Winter was approaching. Soon, Tommy would no longer be able to sit on the front lawn. He would no longer be able to relieve himself outdoors.

The veterinarian showed me how to express his bladder. Locating it with her fingers, she squeezed gently. Tommy squatted and peed on the ground. I bought pee pads, unfolded one on the balcony, and led Tommy over it. When I pressed on his bladder, he peed on the pad. I applauded our small victory. The pads worked well. Large and absorbent, they trapped all the stream.

Every day, I came home for lunch, fed Tommy, and expressed his bladder. Afterward, we sat next to each other on the floor, where I petted him, and sang to him before returning to the office.

The balcony had one drawback. It was a step lower than the floor. Helping Tommy clear the step put a strain on my back. I had to find him another place to urinate. I opened the door of my apartment and unfolded a pad in the hallway. Tommy stepped over the pad, squatted, and peed. A neighbor who saw us grinned; she too had an old dog.

# Chapter 4

Inside the park, however, the dogs and I felt rejuvenated. We were younger, stronger, and healthier than we could remember.

"Look at us," I exclaimed. "How did we get so young, and so healthy all of a sudden?"

"Who knows," said Bobby, "but I sure like this park."

"What is even more surprising," said Tommy, "is that Bobby and I can speak and understand the English language. How cool is that?"

I must have betrayed an air of skepticism.

"We understand English," he repeated, nodding to press his point. Then, he recited the alphabet from beginning to end.

"I agree," said Bobby. "We understand how letters combine to make words, and how words combine to make sentences. We also understand how nouns represent things or events, and how verbs convey action or a state of affairs. Before, we could only understand the tone of your voice, and we could only respond by barking, panting or wagging our tails. But now, we can think and talk, just like you."

I asked, "How do I know that you can think and talk? Say something intelligent to me."

"About what?"

"About the universe. Tell me something about the universe that I don't know."

"Very well," said Tommy. "I believe that the universe is composed of life and form. Without life, form is lifeless. Without form, life is formless. Life meets form to create all things."

There was a pause, and then I said, "I knew that."

"I'm afraid I have a confession to make," I added.

Puzzled, Bobby asked, "A confession? What confession? Why should you confess to us?"

"I'm afraid I've been manipulating you all your lives." Tommy and Bobby raised their eyebrows. "It's true," I insisted. "I made you do things for me by manipulating you, instead of forcing you."

Confused, they stared at me.

"Let me give you an example. Do you remember all the times you laid on my couch in the living room?"

"Yes," replied Bobby. "Almost every day."

"Well, I disapproved. Once you stretched your legs, there was no room for me. Instead of forcing you to leave the couch, I lured you off the couch by going into the kitchen and giving you a treat. Then, I hurried to the couch to steal your spot."

"Really?"

"Yes, really. Sometimes, you took the treat and ran back to the couch before me. Not to worry. I lured you off the couch again by giving you another treat from the kitchen, then stole your spot on the couch. I was manipulating you. Get it?"

I looked for a reaction, then added, “Maybe I should give you another example. When we went for a walk, you often stopped. Instead of pulling you forward with the leash, I lured you forward with a treat from my pocket. I was manipulating you. Now, do you understand? Do you accept my apology?”

“Of course,” said Bobby, “but only if you accept mine.”

Now, I was the one who was confused. “What do you mean?”

“I too have been manipulating you all my life,” he said. “Do you remember all the times I laid on the couch and stretched my legs?”

“Yes, almost every day.”

“I wanted you to give me a treat. Instead of barking, or biting your leg, I laid on the couch and stretched my legs, knowing that you would lure me off the couch by going into the kitchen and giving me a treat. Sometimes, after receiving a treat, I wanted another one. Not to worry. I hurried to the couch before you could steal my spot, and waited until you lured me off the couch with another treat from the kitchen. Also, on our walks, when I wanted a treat, I just stopped, knowing that you would lure me forward with a treat from your pocket.”

Bobby paused, and asked me, “I have more bad news for you. Are you listening?”

“Yes.”

“Not only did I manipulate you to get treats, I also manipulated you to steal your spot on the couch.”

“That’s not possible!” I exclaimed.

Bobby guffawed, then said, “Sometimes, when I wanted to steal your spot on the couch, I looked for something that was dear to you like a shoe, a shirt, a sock, a book, or a pen. The floor was always littered with things that didn't belong there. I grabbed one of them with my teeth, walked in front of you, growled to get your full attention, and shook it violently, knowing that you would jump off the couch to take it from me. Then, I hurried to the couch, and stole your spot."

"How dare you!" I said.

"I know. How devious of me. Can you possibly forgive me?"

"I suppose so," I replied.

# Chapter 5

"How old am I?" asked Tommy.

"You're fifteen years old," I replied.

"How old am I?" asked Bobby.

"You're seven years old."

"How old are you?" they asked.

I did some arithmetic in my head, and replied, "Nine years old."

"Are we brothers?"

"No. You have different parents."

"How long have we lived with you?"

"All your lives. I adopted both of you when you were puppies."

"How did you find us?"

"Let me start with you, Tommy. I have a brother named Pierre, and he convinced me. He always loved dogs. When he was a baby, he learned to bark before he learned to speak, and for years, he barked whenever he saw a dog. I have cousins who grew up with dogs, and when Pierre was a teenager, he spent weekends and summers at their cottage to be with the dogs. Then, one day, he learned that he was allergic to them, and would never be able to live with them. He was disappointed, but never lost his love for them."

“He was married with three children, whereas I was single with no children. We lived near each other, and I spent a lot of time at his house. Maybe he wanted me to visit him less often. ‘You need to get yourself a dog,’ he said. ‘A dog is a wonderful companion. It does whatever you ask, listens to whatever you say, and goes wherever you go.’ I found excuses to decline. I was too busy at work. I went to places that prohibited dogs, like golf courses and ski hills. I ran my own business and worked long hours. How could I possibly fit a dog into my schedule?”

“Then one morning, Pierre asked me again. This time, I hesitated, and replied, ‘Maybe one day.’ I thought I had dodged the question, but I saw his eyes widen. He stood up, and excused himself, claiming that he had errands to run. As he left, he invited me for dinner, and I accepted.”

“I spent the afternoon running errands myself, and when I returned to his house for dinner, I met him on a swing in his backyard. He was cradling something furry in his arms. ‘Meet Tommy,’ he said, ‘your new puppy.’”

“My new puppy!” I gasped. “I never told you to get me a puppy.”

“Sure, you did.”

“No, no. What I said was ‘maybe one day’.”

“Pierre cupped his hands over Tommy’s ears. ‘Claude was only kidding,’ he whispered. ‘He didn’t mean to hurt your feelings.’ Turning to me, he said, ‘I think you owe Tommy an apology.’ Standing up, he handed me the ball of fur.”

I smiled. “I must admit he is cute. How did you decide on a name?””

“Tommy is the name of my favorite clothing store.”

I was disappointed. I had hoped for a name to honor a hero in his life. Still, the name appealed to me, and I kept it.

"You awoke, sighed, and stretched. Pierre knelt on one knee and put you on the ground. You ran to smell the deck, the flower beds, and the cedar trees. You were so small that you had to jump over blades of grass. Then, we went to the garage, and Pierre showed me a crate, toys, and treats he had bought for you. We put you inside the crate and gave you a chewing toy. During the meal, I kept to myself, thinking of the duties I would be assuming, and the freedoms I would be sacrificing."

"After dinner, Pierre took me aside, and said, 'All I ask is that you try. Spend the night with Tommy. See how you feel about him tomorrow morning. If you refuse to keep him, I'll return him to the breeder.'"

"All right,' I said, 'I'll try. He and I shook hands, and I went home. I assembled the crate in the kitchen, then put you inside the crate. I sat on a couch in the den to read. The den was next to the kitchen, and I could see you from the couch. When I took a break to rest my eyes, I looked at the crate and caught you staring at me. At bedtime, I decided to sleep on the couch. When I turned off the light, I looked at the crate and saw you staring at me. In the middle of the night, I went to the kitchen to get a glass of water. You were staring at me. When I got up the next morning, you sat up and wagged your tail to greet me. But there were stools in the crate, and your tail swept them all over the kitchen floor. I opened the gate. You stepped out of the crate, squatted, and peed on the floor."

“*Enough is enough,* I thought, cleaning up the mess. When I called Pierre, he seemed glum, and said, ‘I guess you want me to return Tommy to the breeder.’”

“‘No, not at all,’ I replied. ‘He’s so adorable. Do you know that he spent the entire night staring at me? I think I love him already. I’m keeping him.’”

Bobby laughed, and asked, “How did you find me?”

I smiled. “Actually, you’re the one who found me.”

“Really?”

I nodded. “When Tommy was older, I decided that he should have a companion. I was hoping to adopt a new puppy from Tommy’s mother, but the breeder had retired after her first pregnancy.”

“Pierre recommended another breeder whose dog had just delivered a litter of eight newborn puppies, all Labrador Retrievers.”

“I made an appointment to meet him at his farm. When I arrived, he led me inside a barn to a cage full of puppies. He opened the gate, and the puppies jumped out of the cage, scattering on the ground like mice.”

“There are eight puppies,” he said, “five males and three females. The females have already been adopted. But you can adopt any of the five males.”

As I watched the puppies, I asked him, “They’re all adorable. How can I pick just one of them?”

“He thought for a moment, then said, ‘Instead of picking the puppy, let the puppy pick you.’ I followed him to the front of the barn, where he asked me to sit on the ground. He went inside the barn and reappeared with all five puppies. Placing them at my feet, he invited me to watch their reaction. They all hovered around me like bees, sniffing my pants, and climbing over my legs."

"Then, one of the puppies rubbed himself against my leg, turned in circles, snuggled against it, and fell asleep. Once in a while, he stood up, turned around, snuggled, and resumed his sleep. I watched his rib cage expand and contract with each breath. I petted him gently. He sighed. Meantime, the other puppies wandered away, one by one. The breeder lifted the sleeping puppy and put him back with his brothers a few feet away, but he hopped right back to me."

"I turned to the breeder, smiled, and said, 'I see what you mean. This puppy has just picked me.'"

"We went to the house and sat at a picnic table in the backyard. He reviewed the paperwork and then showed me where to sign. 'What name will you give your puppy?" he asked.

"'Bobby,' I said, 'in honor of my cousin who died tragically in a fire.' We bade each other farewell. In the car, I placed you on my lap and drove home. You slept the whole way."

There was a pause. "What about you, Claude?" asked Tommy.

"I don't remember."

"Did your parents ever tell you?"

"No."

"I know," said Bobby.

"How could you possibly know? You weren't there."

Undaunted, Bobby winked at Tommy, and said, "Once upon a time, there was a young couple who decided to go on a picnic in the countryside. The sky was blue, and the sun was bright. They drove until they saw a majestic tree near the road. They parked the car, unfolded a blanket under the tree, spread their lunch on the blanket, and began to eat."

I looked at Tommy and shook my head, but Bobby continued. "The man and the woman heard a whining sound from the ditch on the side of the road. They got up to look around, and after a while, noticed a hairy thing at the bottom of the ditch. Thinking that it might be an injured monkey, they wrapped it in a blanket and drove to the nearest animal clinic. The man showed it to a veterinarian who asked what it was. He replied that it might be a monkey. The veterinarian looked at the thing from various angles, shook her head, and said, 'Oh dear, that thing is too ugly to be a monkey.'" Tommy smiled.

"'We found it in a ditch,' said the man. 'It might be injured. Can you examine it? We'll pay.'"

"The veterinarian agreed. After conducting her examination, she confirmed that the thing was healthy. The man asked if they could leave it at the clinic. She refused and suggested that they take it to an animal shelter. She gave directions."

"When the man and the woman arrived at the shelter, they spoke to its manager who bragged about accepting all animals in need, even ugly monkeys. But when she pulled back the blanket and took a peek, she recoiled. Pinching her nose, she said, 'Oh dear, that thing stinks too much to be a monkey. Leave my shelter now, before I get sick.'"

"As directed, the man and the woman left the shelter with the thing. During the drive home, she inspected the thing and realized that it was not a monkey after all. It was a boy, an ugly, stinking baby boy. Since nobody else wanted it, she decided to keep it and give it a name. Can you guess what name?"

Struggling to contain himself, Tommy said, "Yes, but tell me."

"She named it Claude."

"Do you mean this Claude?" Grinning, Bobby nodded.

The two dogs dissolved into laughter. At first, I was offended, but their laughter was contagious. My mood changed, and I started to laugh with them.

# Chapter 6

"What else should we talk about?" I asked.

"I know," said Tommy, "but before I tell you, I want you to promise me that you won't laugh."

"I promise."

"I think we're in paradise." I laughed.

There was an awkward silence, then Tommy said, "I'm serious. After all, what is paradise? It must be somewhere I'm completely happy. But no matter how happy I am anywhere, I'll be happier if you're both with me."

Tommy saw my eyes glaze over, and added, "You see, my idea of paradise is hiking in the woods. But no matter how happy I am hiking in the woods, I'll be happier if you're both hiking in the woods with me."

"I get it," said Bobby. "My idea of paradise is swimming in a lake. But no matter how happy I am swimming in a lake, I'll be happier if you're both swimming in the lake with me."

"What does being in paradise have to do with hiking and swimming?" I asked.

"These are just examples," replied Bobby. "Let me find one that suits you. I'm sure that your idea of paradise is lounging on the couch. But no matter how happy you are lounging on the couch, you'll be happier if we're both lounging on the couch with you."

"Now, I see," I said.

There was a pause, then I added, "I'm not sure if we're in paradise, but I am sure I've been here before. You see, I know this park. When I was a kid, my friends and I played in it. We climbed the trees, swam in the pool, and played hockey inside the arena. We went on amusement rides at the summer fair and slid down a long slide at the winter carnival."

"We also lived in houses on streets around the park."

I walked to a maple tree, examined it closely, and added, "This tree was our favorite tree to climb. It was the tallest tree in the park, and it's still the tallest tree."

I paused, and added, "In fact, it's the very same tree."

"How many years ago?"

"Fifty years ago."

"How do you know it's the same tree?"

"The tree has not aged in fifty years. Time hasn't affected it. It's the same tree, with the same trunk, the same branches, and the same leaves. I'm not saying that it's the same tree fifty years later. I'm saying that it's the same tree fifty years ago." I looked around me. "In fact, this entire park, and everything in it has not aged, as if frozen in time for fifty years."

"I happen to know that today, the park looks very different. I doubt you would even recognize it. The arena was replaced by two arenas. The tennis courts were replaced by an indoor swimming pool. The railway tracks were removed, and the railway station was demolished."

I sighed, then said, “I know that what I’m about to say will sound incredible, but I firmly believe that we’ve traveled back in time to the town I knew as a boy, as it was then.” It was Bobby’s turn to laugh.

“I’m serious,” I insisted. “I bet that beyond this park is my boyhood house, and my boyhood town, as they were then.” Tommy became withdrawn and pensive.

“What are you thinking?” I asked.

He looked at me, and said, “Now that we know where we are, we need to ask ourselves why. Why are we revisiting your past? Is there a reason?”

“Who knows,” I said, shrugging my shoulders.

Bobby was becoming restless and said, “I think we should start by revisiting your past. We can ask why later. Claude, tell us about your family.”

“Sure,” I said. “My parents have four children, all boys. In order of age, they are Claude, John, Luc, and Pierre.”

“What is the age difference among you?”

“I’m the oldest. John is eleven months younger than me; Luc was six years younger; and Pierre is eight years younger. We used to live in a house beyond these trees. It must still be there.”

At the end of the park, there was a path that led to a street. As we walked along the path, I looked up and down the street, and felt a strong sense of déjà vu. The cars were bulky and encrusted with chrome. The houses were small but clean, and the yards were well-groomed. There were driveways and cars parked in them, but no garages.

A station wagon pulled into one of the driveways. A man wearing a cap and a uniform stepped out of the car and placed two milk bottles next to the door of a house.

I pointed to a bungalow with white clapboard siding. The roof was covered with blue shingles. A thin strip of navy-blue paint highlighted the front door, the windows and the eaves. On the façade of the house, there were two large windows, and between them, a small window and a front door. Under the door, there was a concrete balcony with steps leading to a concrete sidewalk.

"This was my boyhood home," I began. "The living room is behind the right window. The master bedroom is behind the left window. The bathroom is behind the small window. The kitchen is behind the living room. The den and a second bedroom are behind the master bedroom."

The front door swung open, and a boy ran out of the house. He jumped off the balcony, landed on the sidewalk, and grabbed a hockey stick on the ground. It was made of wood, not fancy aluminum, carbon, or titanium. He started to stickhandle a tennis ball on the concrete path.

"Notice how the blade of the hockey stick is straight," I said.

"Back then, the blades weren't curved as they are today."

"What is so special about the curved blade?"

"It lets you shoot the ball harder."

I stared at the boy and quivered. He had a slim build. His hair was light brown, clean, and short. He noticed me staring at him. "Hello," he said, "do I know you?" I recognized his voice, unmistakably mine at the same age.

"I think I know you," I replied.

"I have no idea who you are."

There was a white picket fence surrounding an above-ground pool that was circular in shape.

Pointing at the fence, I said, "I helped my father build this fence. I also helped him paint it."

"No, I'm the one who helped him."

"Dad and I also swam in this pool at night," I continued. "When everyone else in the house was asleep, he woke me up and asked me to follow him to the pool. We had to be quiet because John was asleep in the next bed. We tiptoed out of the house, opened the gate, slipped inside the pool, and glided on the surface, pushing ourselves along the bottom. Pretending to be a crocodile, I growled for special effect."

"Crocodiles growl," said Bobby. "And all this time I thought they hissed. Who knew."

"Then, we sat against the wall of the pool and talked. Usually, he asked me about my day. Hoping to extend our time together, I talked and talked, recalling the smallest detail of my day. He also asked me about school. Was I getting along with the teacher and my classmates? Was I keeping up with my homework? Did I have deadlines to meet? He never allowed me to speak ill of anyone. If I criticized someone, he told me to say something nice. If I criticized someone of authority, like a priest, he reminded me of my duty to respect him. When it was time to go, he made me promise not to tell anyone, put a towel around me, and led me inside the house. My souvenirs of these midnight swims with Dad are among my happiest."

Mesmerized, the boy smiled, and his eyes brightened. I knew that I had touched his soul. I had described details that only he and his father knew. The swims had occurred in the middle of the night, while the rest of the family slept. And the boy kept his promise not to tell anyone. He realized that his father and my father were one and the same person, and therefore, that he and I were one and the same person.

"I am you fifty years from now," I said, "and you are me fifty years ago."

Baffled at first, he quickly regained his composure, and said, "I can't be you. You're old, and I'm young."

"I was young when I was ten years old, and you'll be old when you're sixty."

"Maybe, but you're bald. I have a head with hair."

"I had a head of hair when I was ten, and you'll be bald when you're sixty."

"But you're fat. I'm thin."

"I was thin when I was ten, and you'll be fat when you're sixty."

He took a closer look at me. "But you're ugly."

"Enough with the comparisons."

"You must be lost. Where did you come from? How did you get here?"

I shrugged my shoulders. "Your guess is as good as mine."

The dogs panted and wagged their tails in delight. "Meet Tommy and Bobby," I said.

"Can you talk to us about your father?" said Tommy.

I shrugged my shoulders and said, "I know very little about his early life. Whenever I asked him, he refused to answer. Over the years, I learned that he was one of ten children, and lived in a small village. His mother died when he was young. He received his primary education in a one-room brick house, heated by a wood stove. He attended high school in the next village, five miles away. As there were no school buses, he walked the distance between the two villages every weekday. He attended university in a large city and graduated with a bachelor's degree. Afterward, he became a schoolteacher, returned to his father's house, and taught all the village children, including his younger siblings."

"He was a strict disciplinarian and expected all the pupils to do their homework. He made no exception for his siblings. Each morning, he reviewed all the workbooks. Once, he admonished two of his sisters for neglecting to do their homework the night before. After school, they complained to their father who promptly confronted him, and warned him never to embarrass his siblings again, lest he pull them out of school, or better still, evict him from his house."

"My father started as a schoolteacher, became a school inspector, then ended his career as a senior officer in the provincial government, accountable only to the Minister of his department. He attributed all his achievements to his formal education."

# Chapter 7

I turned to the boy and asked, "Is your mother inside the house?" He nodded. I felt the urge to go inside, introduce myself to her, chat with her, and thank her for rearing me. I never became rich or famous in life, but because of the tools that she and my father had given me, I was able to earn a good living by pursuing the profession of my choice.

Then, I imagined her coming out the door and surprising me, an old man accosting her ten-year-old son in the front yard of her own house. She would suspect that I was trying to lure him, kidnap him, and harm him. And how could I explain my presence? How could I claim to be her son from the future? I was twice her age. She would chase me off her property, pull her son inside the house, and report me to the police. I resolved to leave the property before she appeared at the door, but Tommy distracted me. Now, he was curious to learn more about my mother.

"She was one of the most resilient people I ever knew," I began. "She and my father survived the Great Depression and the Second World War. She was tough, not mouthy or pushy, just able to overcome adversity. She came from a large family that was poor, but highly educated. Her mother had thirteen children. As an older child, she was expected to help her mother take care of the younger children."

"She was our primary caregiver. She did the housework and took care of us. She bathed us, dressed us, fed us, washed our clothes, and organized our activities. One day, I tried to wear the same pair of socks two days in a row. She caught me and made me change my socks, explaining that if I ever hurt myself, and required medical care, she wanted the doctor to think that I had a good mother. Her main objective in life was to prepare her children for life as adults. She monitored our school homework and piano practices. She had an unwavering faith in our abilities and reminded us that we could accomplish any goal we set if we applied ourselves. She always made time for us."

"She had grown up in a city and was taught by Catholic nuns who had exacting standards, and singled out lazy pupils. To avoid criticism, she always completed her assignments on time."

"Both my parents came from poor families and were taught to be thrifty. They knew how to stretch a dollar. When they bought us things to wear, like shoes and clothes, they picked things that were a few sizes too large, so we could grow into them."

Suddenly, a pretty woman in her thirties stepped outside the house. I froze and stared at her in awe. She had a pretty face, a smooth complexion, and long dark hair tied at the back in a ponytail. She wore a white shirt with a straight cut that hung loosely over her waist, pants that fit tightly around her legs, and plain white sneakers. My jaw dropped. I was staring at my own mother, except she was half my age.

"Hello," I said sheepishly.

But she neither saw me nor heard me. “It’s time for you to practice the piano,” she told the boy.

“Just give me five more minutes,” he pleaded. She nodded and went back inside the house.

The boy and I looked at each other and shrugged our shoulders. “Mom thought I was alone,” he said. “She had no idea that you and the dogs were with me. You were invisible to her.”

He dropped his hockey stick and walked to a willow tree in the front yard. It had a large trunk that split into three separate boughs a few feet above the ground. The boughs supported a thick spray of branches, twigs, and leaves.

“Watch me,” he said. “Today, I’ll break my record. I’ll climb higher than ever before.” He glanced at the house, spit in his hands, and rubbed them together. Then, he pulled himself up the tree, one branch at a time. The branches hardly moved when he put his weight on them. Within seconds, he was near the top, where the boughs turned into branches, and the branches turned into twigs.

Facing the dogs, I said, “As a boy, I climbed this tree when I had no time to go to the park. But my parents disapproved because they were afraid I would hurt myself. If they saw me in the tree, they ordered me to come down and threatened to punish me the next time I was caught. But I knew better. They were just talking.”

The boy paused to look around him. The tree swayed under his weight. “It’s a bit windy,” he said, “but I’ll try anyway.”

I knew what was coming, and tried to prevent it. “I think you should come down. You’ll hurt yourself.” He ignored me. I walked up to the tree, planted my feet firmly on the ground, and extended my arms, waiting.

He reached for a twig and held it gently between his fingers. He tried to pull himself higher, but the twig bent under his weight. With the other hand, he reached for another twig. The twigs under his feet broke, leaving him dangling in the air. The twigs under his hands broke, and he fell. I tried to catch him to break his fall, but he slipped through my fingers and landed on the ground with a heavy thud, one of his legs caught in the crotch of the tree.

He groaned and struggled to catch his breath. Then, he slowly dislodged his leg and stood up. His body was covered in scrapes.

"Are you all right?" I asked.

Wincing, he nodded and brushed himself off in a hurry.

His mother rushed out of the house, and asked, "What happened? Are you hurt?"

"No, Mom."

"Were you climbing the tree?"

The boy just shrugged his shoulders. "Go to Luc's bedroom. Let me have a good look at you. Then, you can practice the piano." The boy began to writhe in mock agony.

"Stop faking," she said.

As he was climbing the stairs, he turned to me, and asked, "Do you want to come inside the house?"

"Are you asking me?"

"No, Mom. I was just talking to myself." They disappeared inside the house.

Bobby looked at me and said, "I should apologize."

"Why?"

"I was unfair earlier when I said you were a monkey."

"I accept your apology."

"I don't think you understand. I don't owe you an apology. I owe monkeys an apology. I was unfair to them, not to you. Monkeys are agile, nimble, and graceful. They swing from branch to branch effortlessly. But you fell down the tree like a sack of potatoes. Comparing you to a monkey was unfair to monkeys. I hope they can forgive me."

# Chapter 8

The dogs and I were standing next to the picket fence. "I learned to swim in this pool," I said.

"You call pushing yourself along the bottom of the pool swimming?" asked Bobby.

"I'll have you know that I'm an expert swimmer. I've known how to swim all my life. My brother John and I took lessons from the Red Cross at the pool in the park. We also took lessons at a summer camp. We learned all the strokes. We were tested, and earned badges, which our mother sewed on our swimsuits."

"What was John like?" asked Tommy.

"He and I grew up together. Although he was eleven months younger than me, he was bigger and stronger. He had long arms and broad shoulders. In all the family pictures, he was taller by a few inches, which annoyed me because everyone thought he was the senior. He was an accomplished swimmer and gymnast."

"When John and I were teenagers, my parents bought a big house. They hired a contractor to build an inground pool in the backyard. From the dining room window, I watched the workers dig a hole in the ground, lay a web of steel mesh in the hole, and pour concrete over the mesh. The pool had a deep and shallow end joined together by a gradual slope. I swam in the pool every day. Mornings, I dove into the water instead of taking a shower. Sometimes, John and I raced each other."

I paused for a few seconds, then added, "One night, I even saved John from drowning."

Bobby looked at me suspiciously. "In the shallow end?" he asked.

"No, the deep end."

People are vain. They worry about how other people perceive them. They worry about how family members perceive them because they live with them, and they worry about how friends perceive them because they socialize with them. I'm no exception.

In the hope of impressing my dogs, I proceeded to tell them a story, true in every detail, except one.

"One night after dinner," I began, "John and I were alone in the house. I was fifteen years old, and he was fourteen. My parents had gone to an event together and taken Pierre with them. In the basement, there were two rooms, a playroom with a pool table, and a kitchenette with a fridge stacked with beer, which they kept for their friends. John and I were playing pool when we started to talk about beer."

"'Have you ever tasted beer?' asked John."

"Sure, many times. I like beer. Hey! Let's drink the beer in the fridge. Mom and Dad won't notice a few empty bottles."

"I opened the fridge door, grabbed two bottles, opened them, and gave one to John. I took a sip from mine and grimaced. I took another sip, shivered, gagged, and felt the hair on my neck rise. I looked away, so John wouldn't see me."

"'I love beer,' I said. 'It tastes so good. I can't wait to be old enough to drink beer legally.' I held my breath and took another sip, which I almost heaved up."

"John noticed me and said, 'I thought you liked beer.'"

"Nodding, I replied, 'I do, but this beer is a little too cold for me. I prefer my beer warm.' I pretended to take sips, but when I put the bottle to my lips, I blocked the spout with my tongue. Then, I smacked my lips in mock delight. After a few minutes, I found an excuse to leave the kitchenette. 'Beer makes me hungry,' I said."

"I went upstairs, emptied my bottle in the kitchen sink, took a bag of chips, and returned to the basement. I showed John my empty beer bottle. 'Do you want another beer?' I asked, opening the fridge door."

"John nodded, and asked, 'Did you finish drinking your first beer already?' He downed his beer and handed me the empty bottle."

I gave him another bottle. 'Do you want chips?' I asked. 'I like chips with my beer.'

"John refused, saying, 'No. I like beer with my beer.'"

"At one point, John went to the bathroom. When he was gone, I emptied the beer inside my bottle into his bottle. When John came back, I gave him his bottle and showed him my empty bottle."

"John downed his bottle again, then took two other bottles from the fridge, opened one, and gave me the other. I took a sip from mine. I held my breath, and to my surprise, managed to keep it down without grimacing. The beer tasted a little better. The alcohol was dulling my taste buds.

I felt lightheaded, but John looked inebriated. He wore a glazed expression and slurred his words. We started to giggle for no reason."

"I stumbled into the playroom, looked at the clock, and shouted, 'Oh no, I lost track of time. Mom and Dad will be here any minute. We have to stop drinking beer, and sober up.' John and I emptied the beer bottles down the drain and stacked them in a case. 'Let's go for a swim in the pool,' I suggested."

"We staggered to the pool in the backyard. John undressed, walked to the edge in his underwear, and dove into the deep end."

"The water was about eight feet deep. Bubbles rose to the surface. Several seconds passed. He was still down at the bottom of the pool, and the bubbles were still rising. I dove after him, wrapped my arms around his chest, and pulled him to safety. I'm quite sure that I saved his life."

"I'm quite dubious," said the boy.

I looked up. I had forgotten all about him. He was standing at the window of Luc's bedroom, overlooking the side yard.

"Is Claude telling us the truth?" asked Bobby.

"The story is true, but not the ending. When John dives into the pool, he'll come out refreshed. But when Claude dives, his head will hit the bottom. Stunned, he'll rise slowly to the top. John will see he's in trouble, dive into the water, and pull him to safety. It will be John who rescues Claude, not Claude who rescues John."

I was speechless. The boy's recollection of the ending had been perfect. But how could he know? He hadn't experienced the incident yet. He wouldn't experience it for years to come.

"Did Claude put a hole in the pool when he hit his head on the bottom?" asked Bobby.

Sometimes, when people are caught fibbing, they recover from the initial embarrassment to tell a second fib. The benefit of improving their image is so alluring, and the risk of getting caught is so minimal that they take another chance, doing their best to look sincere. Of course, the second fib is uncovered, and their image suffers another blow.

"But I can swim," I insisted. "Let me tell you another story, one that will convince you, I'm sure. Once, I was forced to swim in freezing cold rapids to save myself from drowning. It was early in the spring. I went canoeing with friends in a provincial park for the weekend. There were eight of us, six experts and two novices. I was one of the novices. As a boy, I had paddled a canoe on a gentle lake, but never in frigid whitewater fed by melting snow. We arrived at the park on Friday afternoon and pitched our tents. After dinner, we packed our canoes and went to bed. On the next morning, we enjoyed a hearty breakfast and carried the canoes to the water. In their wisdom, the experts paired the novices in the same canoe. 'Just watch us,' they said, 'and do what we do.'"

"The experts shoved off the shore, then the novices shoved off the shore. My friend sat in the front, and I sat in the back. We drifted on the water for a few minutes, and looked around, admiring the view. The sky was clear, the air was crisp, and the water was still. The ground was bare, except for patches of snow near the banks. The sun's rays danced on the water. I felt relaxed, one with nature, and took a series of deep breaths to savor the moment."

"Little did I know that my friend was a field naturalist. 'This park,' he began, 'has two sides, the east side and the west side. We're on the west side, a forest of hardwood trees interspersed with softwoods.'"

"He pointed to a tree, and added, 'That tree is a sugar maple, the most common tree in the park. It produces maple syrup, and its leaf is displayed on the Canadian flag. In the summer, the leaves are green and yellow, but in the fall, they turn orange and red.'"

"He looked around him, and added, 'Look at the cluster of bright white birches over there. The bark is papery. It was used by natives to build canoes.'"

"'And do you see the tree with the smooth grey bark on the hill? It's an American beech. There is a nest at the top of the tree. Bears made that nest.'"

"How?" I asked.

"'The tree produces beechnuts that black bears love. They climb up the tree, sit in a crotch, and bend the branches above them to reach the beechnuts. If the branches break, they either fall on the ground or gather in the crotch to form a nest.'"

"He raised his arms toward the sky, took another deep breath, and pointed to a scruffy tree near the edge of the water, whose branches were short and drooping. 'The branches of the black spruce are very strong. In the winter, they can support large loads of snow without breaking.'"

"Suddenly, the canoe began to wobble. I looked ahead and saw rocks protruding from the surface. Water crashed on the rocks, and mixed with air to form whitewater. The current became stronger."

"Ahead of us, the experts alerted each other of upcoming hazards and paddled from side to side to avoid them. They shouted strange words like 'bow', 'stern', 'port', and 'starboard', which we shouted ourselves to no avail. The canoe bounced among the rocks like a metal ball inside a pinball machine. All our efforts to steady the canoe made it wobble even more. Finally, we surrendered to the elements, threw the oars in the canoe, and grabbed both sides in a combined effort to keep it afloat."

"The canoe became wedged between two rocks, causing it to lurch. We nearly fell overboard. The current dislodged the canoe and sent it downstream. A rock cracked the hull. Water started oozing into the canoe."

"We became entangled in overhanging branches. We tried to push them away, but leaned on the same side, and capsized the canoe."

The freezing water overwhelmed me. I lost my breath and felt my chest constrict. I pointed my feet downstream and floated on my back. Water splashed all around me. I tried to take short breaths, but every time I opened my mouth, water poured into it. My hands and feet went numb. I thought I might be on the verge of drowning. "But I mustered all my strength, and managed to swim to the shore."

I looked at the dogs for signs of admiration. Instead, I saw signs of skepticism. "Is Claude exaggerating again?" asked Bobby.

“A little,” he replied. “When he falls into the water, Claude won’t have to swim. The water will only be four feet deep. He’ll plant his feet in the bed of the river, stand up and walk to shore.”

# Chapter 9

Bobby turned to Tommy, and said, "It seems to me that whenever Claude goes into the water, he either touches the bottom or sinks to the bottom. One thing he does not do is swim. Unlike me."

"I swim like a fish."

Tommy nodded. Emboldened by flattery, Bobby continued, "I remember my first time in the water. We went to a cottage on a lake. As soon as we arrived, I jumped out of the car, ran to the lake, and dove into the water, making a big splash. I was about five feet from the shore. My neck outstretched, I flapped my front paws and kicked my hind legs. I couldn't feel the bottom."

"You weren't really swimming," I said. "You were treading water."

"Eventually," said Bobby, "I did find the shore. I shook the water off my back. There were guests on the deck, and I heard them clap. So, I hopped on the deck, weaved around them until I reached the end, and dove into the water again, this time twenty feet from the shore. I zigzagged along the surface until I found the shore. The guests gave me a standing ovation."

"They were standing on the deck because there were no chairs on the deck."

"A few weeks later," said Tommy, "we went back to the cottage. Claude pitched a tennis ball in the lake. You dove, fetched it, and swam back to shore. Your paws splashed the water, your ears flapped up and down, but you swam in a straight line. You continued to fetch the ball, and each time, you kicked harder, splashed less water, and swam faster. Soon, you were gliding along the surface, and only your ears were flapping up and down."

Bobby said, "If only the guests had been there to see me."

Tommy said, "I also remember the time you swam in rough water. Near the apartment, there was a footpath that extended along a river on one side and a street on the other. Usually, Claude kept us on a leash to prevent us from wandering in the street. But at one point, the street gave way to a fence along the back of rowhouses. Thinking that you and I were confined between the river and the fence, Claude untied our leashes."

"While I stayed close to him, you, Bobby, started to run in circles. I thought you had nowhere to go, but I should have known better. You stopped, lifted your head, and gazed at the river as if you were noticing it for the first time. Then, you ran straight for the water, leaped over the bank, and dove into the river. Claude nearly panicked. He had never seen you swim in a river with a strong current. Downstream, the river poured into another river. We were so close that I could hear the falls. Claude had to find a way to pluck you from the water before you drifted over the edge. He went downstream, and stood on the shore, hoping to grab you. But you floated past him. He ran downstream again, and stepped into the water, this time venturing a little further. When he looked up the river, he could only see water. Thinking that you had gone under the surface, he called your name."

"As if I could have barked under the water."

"But you did bark, Bobby. You barked from the shore. Claude was so shocked to see you that he almost lost his balance. 'Stay, stay, stay,' he pleaded. For once, you listened. He walked up to you, and tied the leash to your collar."

Tommy smiled, and said, "Well done."

Frowning, I told Tommy, "I admit that Bobby was a good swimmer. But sometimes he did things in the water that were quite reprehensible. When you were too old to go to the kennel, I kept you both at home during the day. I wanted Bobby to keep you company. But he was still young and needed exercise. I consulted my next-door neighbor who also had a dog. She told me that a dogwalker exercised her dog on weekdays."

"The dogwalker had impeccable credentials. She had lived with dogs all her life. She made a living walking them. She was able to control several dogs at the same time. I asked her where she took them. To a public park, she said, where they played under her supervision."

"I was nervous, but her confidence won me over. She asked me if Bobby was socialized, and I was happy to inform her that he had gone to a daycare kennel all his life. She agreed to take him."

"On the first day, I met her at my apartment. She took Bobby and introduced him to the other dogs inside the van. They greeted him enthusiastically. Then, she waved at me, climbed into her van, and sped away. A few hours later, she returned Bobby home and announced that he and the other dogs had gotten along famously. She looked forward to her next walk with him."

"Unfortunately, her good impression of Bobby crashed on the second walk. She picked him up at the apartment while I was at work. I assumed that the visit had gone well until I arrived home after work, and saw mud splattered on the walls and carpeting of the lobby. I also saw mud splattered on the furniture and bookshelves in my apartment. Bobby jumped on me to greet me and smothered my suit with mud."

"I knocked on my neighbor's door. She confirmed that her dog had also made a mess in her apartment. She called the dogwalker who placed the blame squarely on Bobby. Apparently, all the dogs had been playing in the park until Bobby was enticed away by a mud puddle at the other end of the park. He trotted to the puddle, sat in the middle of it, rolled on his back, and squirmed from side to side, his legs pointed to the sky in glee until his coat was thoroughly saturated. The other dogs saw him and followed his lead. One by one, they took mud baths."

"The dogwalker brought the dogs home in their filthy state. 'If you think your apartment is full of mud,' she told my neighbor, 'you should see my van.'"

"I returned to my apartment and phoned the dogwalker. Before I could apologize, she vented her anger. One client had fired her. Another client demanded compensation.

Then, she fired me unceremoniously, and ended the call abruptly."

"I thought Bobby's groomer would decline to give him a bath and shampoo, but she graciously accepted, and made him look new again."

# Chapter 10

We heard banging noises inside the house. "Good grief," said Bobby, covering his ears. "What a racket. Is someone destroying the piano with a sledgehammer?"

"Excuse me," I said indignantly. "That racket you hear is me, as a boy, playing the piano. I'm practicing Beethoven's Ninth Symphony, one of his finest works. He wrote it after he had lost his hearing."

"If I listen much longer, I'll lose my own hearing."

Undaunted, I said, "When my brother John and I were boys, we took piano lessons. Let's go inside the house, and watch the boy play."

"Are you sure?" asked Tommy.

"Yes. After all, he invited us."

The front door was closed, but we stepped through it effortlessly. The living room was the first room on our right. In front of us, the boy was playing the piano. On our left, there was a stereo cabinet, and on our right, under the living room window, there was a sofa, a coffee table, and a rocking chair. I lifted the lid of the cabinet and saw a turntable, a tonearm, a needle, and a console with dials. Vinyl albums were stacked neatly inside a compartment. One of the sleeves featured Elvis Presley singing, and strumming an acoustic guitar.

Bobby looked at me, and said, “The boy’s wrists are limp. They should be straight and kept level with the keyboard. His fingers should be curved. He stood upright and moved his paws up and down to show us how piano keys should be tapped.”

I looked at Bobby sideways, and asked, “Are you almost finished?”

“How often did you practice the piano?” asked Tommy.

“Fifteen minutes every day. If I missed a practice one day, I had to make it up the next day. If I went away for a weekend, I had to make up two extra days of practice.”

The boy heard us and turned around. “I’m rehearsing for a concert to be held at the convent,” he said.

“What is a convent?” Bobby asked me.

“It’s a residence for Catholic nuns. Nuns are women of the Catholic faith who have given vows of poverty, chastity, and obedience. They live a cloistered life of prayer and charity inside a convent.”

“I’m sorry I asked.”

“John and I took piano lessons at the convent for years. One of the nuns was our teacher. Every Saturday morning, she taught us one at a time. First, we did our scales, then performed a piece of classical music that we had practiced all week at home. At the end of the practice, she gave us a new piece to learn during the following week.”

“I enjoyed going to the convent. Taking piano lessons relaxed me, and energized me. It improved my mood and memory. It also inspired me to study harder and perform better at school. Music was an important part of my education."

The boy stopped playing and turned around. "I can hear you," he said. "Did you say piano lessons relax me? Are you kidding? The truth is that I like going to the convent, not because I play the piano for an hour, but because I run and slide across the hardwood floor during the other hour, while John plays the piano. Before the lessons, the nun waxes her floor. When John and I arrive at the convent, she gives us slippers to wear. While she teaches one of us, the other one runs around the room. I hate the hour that I play the piano, but I love the hour that I run across the floor. As you can imagine, after two hours, the floor looks really shiny." The boy turned around and resumed his practice.

I nodded, and said, "I suppose he's right. I remember the joy of running in slippers. I ran the whole hour without taking a rest. Nobody had to coax me. I made a game of it. Pretending to be wearing skates, I pushed off the first foot, and slid on the second foot, then pushed off the second foot, and slid on the first foot. When I reached the other side of the room, I turned around and slid across the room again. Occasionally, I veered to avoid an imaginary obstacle. If I slipped and fell, the nun turned around and asked me if I was hurt, but she never asked me to stop skating."

I pulled the dogs aside, and making sure I was out of the boy's earshot, I whispered, "I remember the piano concert that the boy mentioned." The nun had invited several important guests, including the parish priest, the mayor, and the parents. John, another boy, and I played in a trio together. Ours was the opening number. "Unfortunately, the trio was a flop. We bombed. The reason was that the three of us had never practiced the piece together. We knew how to play our individual parts, but we had never blended them together. The first time we played as a trio was on the night of the concert itself."

"After the guests took their seats, the nun introduced us. We walked onstage and took a bow, sat on the bench, paused for a few seconds, and started to play. Things went bad from the beginning. We sounded like musicians tuning their instruments before a concert. We weren't playing in sync at all. I'm sure the guests had no idea what piece we were supposed to be playing. We tried to adjust and even whispered instructions to each other, but nothing worked. So we rushed through our own part of the piece. Soon, we were racing against each other, and making huge mistakes. But we never quit. We soldiered on and finished one after the other."

"The room fell silent. The guests looked nervously at each other, struggling to keep straight faces. We sat still on the bench, afraid to turn and face them. Then, we started to giggle, and the sound of a horn filled the room. One of us had had released gas from the bottom. The guests exploded in laughter. We stood up, turned, and made a hasty exit."

"The concert was not a complete flop. We also had solo pieces of music to play, and we performed them flawlessly. At the end of the evening, when all the performers went on stage to take a bow, the guests, including the nun, reserved their warmest applause for us, I think because we had persevered to the end, despite making so many mistakes."

Bobby said, "Once, I also gave a performance at a concert, but mine was superb."

I guffawed, and asked, "What instrument did you play?"

"Voice," he said. "I was also the conductor. You should remember. You were there. Early one morning, while the neighborhood slept, you and I went for a walk. The streets and sidewalks were deserted. We passed a bus shelter. Soon, it would be full of commuters waiting for a bus to take them to work, but at that time, it was empty. Behind the shelter, there was a tall apartment building, many storeys high, with windows in the front, and balconies at both ends."

"I stopped in front of the building, lifted my head, turned it from side to side slowly, and in my deepest bass voice, barked, 'woh, woh, woh.' I waited a few seconds and barked again, 'Woh, woh, woh.' Inside an apartment, a small dog with a sweet soprano voice barked, 'Wee, wee, wee.' Then, another dog barked, 'Wah, wah, wah.' For a while, we were barking in perfect harmony: 'Wah, wee, woh, woh, wah, wee, woh, wah, wee.' If there was a lull, I barked to revitalize the performance. Then, I stopped to listen, my tongue lolling out."

Bobby shut his eyes to replay the performance in his mind, then opened his eyes, and said, "Soon, the residents inside the apartments took notice. They turned on the lights and looked through the windows. When they saw me, they waved and knocked on the windows to show their appreciation. One resident even shouted from his balcony, probably requesting an encore."

"Unfortunately, Claude decided to leave the concert before the end. He fled down the street with me in tow, depriving the residents of their encore."

# Chapter 11

The living room fell silent. "I finished my practice, Mom," yelled the boy.

"Has it been fifteen minutes already?" she asked.

"Yes."

"Then, come to the den, and memorize your prayers."

"But I can memorize my prayers after lunch."

"After lunch, you'll have to do your homework."

The dogs and I met the boy at the piano. Tommy turned to him, and said, "I know that you and Claude are one and the same person, but I would prefer to call you by different names."

"I'm keeping my name. You can call yourself a different name if you want."

The boy thought, then said, "Call me Andy. It's my middle name, and I prefer it anyway. When I'm old enough to have a boy of my own, I'll call him Andy."

"Then it's settled." Pointing at me, Tommy said, "You're Claude," and pointing at the boy, he said, "You're Andy." We all nodded.

"Follow me to the den," said Andy.

"Why do you have to memorize prayers?" asked Bobby.

Andy hesitated briefly, then said, "The priest suspended me this morning. I was his altar boy at mass. While reciting a prayer in Latin, I forgot one of the verses, and instead of looking stupid, I invented a few sounds that sounded Latin. The parishioners never noticed. They understand Latin less than I do. But the priest noticed. After mass, he took me aside and suspended me. I was humiliated. All my friends are altar boys, and they will ridicule me if they ever find out. I need to learn the prayers to be reinstated as soon as possible."

We walked down the hall and entered the first doorway on the right. There was a hot water radiator against the opposite wall, and a small table and two chairs on the near wall. Andy's mother sat in one chair. She was knitting, and watching television. The other chair was empty.

The television set was against the far wall. It was a large wooden box, not a flat screen, and it flashed images in black and white. I told the dogs, "Color images had not yet been invented." She asked Andy to turn off the set. He walked across the room, turned a knob on the set, and the images vanished. "Remote devices had not been invented either," I added.

Andy sat in the empty chair, grabbed a book on the table, and started reading it.

Tommy looked at me and asked, "What were priests?"

"Priests were the spiritual leaders of our community. They celebrated mass in church and taught various subjects in school. During recess, they played with us in the schoolyard, and evenings, they led meetings of our social clubs, like the Crusaders, and the Cub Scouts. In the summer, they took us camping, and in the winter, they played hockey with us. We admired them, sought their approval, confided in them, and confessed our sins to them. We never challenged their authority. When a priest reprimanded us, we felt embarrassed, and made amends as soon as possible."

I paused and noticed that the dogs were still listening to me. "One Sunday morning," I said, "I was helping a priest celebrate mass. Near the end of the service, he reached inside the tabernacle and removed a goblet of hosts. After consecrating them, he left the altar to give communion to the parishioners, who had formed a row in front of him, from one side of the church to the other. Kneeling, they extended their tongues, received the hosts, and walked back to their seats. But the less faithful among them tried to sneak out of the church early. When the priest saw them, he handed me the goblet, hurried to his pulpit, and shouted into the microphone, 'Mass is not over. Come back to your seats and pray for your souls.' Stunned, the delinquent parishioners turned around and shuffled to their seats. None of them disobeyed the priest."

"What book is Andy reading?" asked Tommy.

"It's a Catechism, a book of prayers in Latin. Andy is memorizing his prayers so he can recite them during mass. In those days, we learned by rote. We memorized."

"What does 'memorize' mean?" asked Tommy.

"We memorize something when we repeat it to ourselves until we can recall it easily. In Science, we memorized the elements and compounds. In Geography, we memorized the countries and capital cities. In history, we memorized the dates of battles. In Math, we memorized multiplication tables. And in religion, we memorized prayers."

"I'm ready, Mom," announced Andy.

"Which one do you want to recite first?"

"The 'Hail Mary'."

She flipped the pages of the Catechism until she found the prayer, and told Andy to start. He took a deep breath and said:

Ave Maria, gratia plena, Dominus tecum.

Benedicta tu mulieribus…

"I don't understand a single word," complained Bobby.

I shrugged my shoulders, and said, "Neither did I. The recitation was in Latin. Nobody understood a single word, except the priests, but we recited our prayers in Latin anyway."

When Andy was finished, his mother asked him to recite 'Our Father.' The recitation was flawless. "Good," she said. "Now, try the 'I Believe in God.'"

Andy hesitated. "I made my mistake with this prayer. I better review it one last time."

She handed him the Catechism and resumed her knitting.

"Are you knitting my wool coat?" he asked her.

"Yes."

"Are you using the pattern with the rocket on the back?"

"Yes. Now, memorize your prayer."

Andy read the prayer, closed his eyes, and recited it under his breath, occasionally peeking at the book for divine inspiration. After a few attempts, he handed the book to his mother. "I'm ready," he said, then began:

"Credo in Deum, Patrem omnipotentem Creatorem caeli et terrae Et in Iesum Christum, Filium eius unicum, Dominum nostrum: Descendo ad inferos…"

"No," she interrupted, "descendit ad inferos."

"That's what I meant," said Andy: "descendit ad inferos, tertia die resurrexit a mortuis, ascendit ad caelos…"

Because Andy had made a mistake, his mother made him repeat his recitation from beginning to end twice.

Before long, Andy had recited all the prayers perfectly and asked to be excused.

His mother nodded.

A few minutes later, Andy ate lunch. When he was finished, his mother reminded him to do his homework.

Andy frowned and said, "But I just finished playing the piano and memorizing the prayers. I'm too tired to do any homework. I need to take a break."

"Did you see the priest on the next morning?" asked Tommy.

"I sure did," said Andy. "As I was reciting the prayers, he kept interrupting. He stopped me halfway through one prayer and asked me to recite another prayer. He began reciting one himself, stopped and then asked me to take over. I complied without hesitation. 'All right,' he said, almost grudgingly, 'You can come back. Check the schedule later today to see when you serve mass again. And don't let me catch you making another mistake.'"

# Chapter 12

Andy, the dogs, and I left the den, walked across the kitchen and stood on a platform. The back door was on one side. A staircase leading to the basement was on the other.

We climbed down the stairs. Andy went to his bedroom, but the dogs and I stopped at the foot of the stairs. I turned around, pointed to the back door, and said, "When he was two years old, my brother Luc was standing next to the door. I was outside and opened the door to enter the house. The door hit Luc and sent him flying in the air. My mother was standing a few steps down the staircase, and caught him before he landed."

"Luc was lucky."

"This time maybe," I said, "but luck was never on his side. On another occasion, he and I were on the front lawn of the house. I was trying to show him how to catch a football. I meant to lob it in his hands, but I mistakenly pitched it in his face, causing him to bite his tongue. Bleeding and crying, he ran inside the house."

Suddenly, I was overwhelmed with sorrow. Tears filled my eyes. I covered them to hide the tears.

"What's wrong?" asked Tommy.

I took a deep breath, and said, "Luc was taken from us when he was only two years old. He drowned at a farmhouse on the outskirts of town."

"What happened?"

"My parents had left him and my youngest brother Pierre at the farmhouse for a weekend, while they took John and me to a city named North Bay, where Dad was scheduled to attend a series of business meetings. North Bay was five hours away by car. John and I were old enough to travel long distances, but Luc and Pierre were too young, so my parents left them in the care of trusted friends, who owned the farmhouse. In the yard, there was a reservoir of water for use by firefighters to extinguish fires at the farm."

"It was a cold afternoon, a few degrees below freezing. One of the owners dressed Luc, and sent him outside, unsupervised. A thin layer of ice covered the water in the reservoir. Luc wandered to the reservoir and stepped on the ice. He fell through it and drowned. He died with his toes pointed, trying to reach the bottom. At the funeral home, he was exposed in his socks because the director had been unable to fit shoes on his feet."

"The rest of the family arrived in North Bay at dinnertime. We unpacked our luggage at a motel and ate a quick meal. After driving us to a movie theatre, Dad went to his meeting. Soon, however, he was back. He went to the front of the theatre, caught our attention, and motioned for us to follow him. He waited until we were inside the car to tell us that Luc had drowned earlier in the day."

"We all burst into tears. On the way home, John and I peppered Dad with questions which he did his best to answer. Eventually, we cried ourselves to sleep. We arrived at the funeral home in the middle of the night, and my father went straight to the basement to identify Luc's body."

"The next morning, we went to the farmhouse to get Pierre. The owners kept apologizing, but my father kept insisting that the drowning had been accidental."

Neither he nor my mother ever expressed any resentment against them.

"For years, I felt guilty about going to North Bay with my parents, instead of staying behind at the farmhouse with Luc. When John and I were younger, we also stayed at the farmhouse. On this occasion, however, my parents felt that we were old enough to accompany them to North Bay. So, they only left Luc and Pierre behind. But I could have insisted on being with them. Had I been there, I would have watched them like a hawk, and neither one of them would have gone anywhere near that reservoir. Luc would still be alive today."

"His drowning was a senseless tragedy. Why did he die so young? Why did his life end before it began? What did he ever do to deserve such a cruel fate? I'm still searching for answers today, but I know I'll never find any."

I paused.

"Claude," shouted Andy. "Where are you? Come into my room. I want to show you something."

The dogs followed me to the bedroom. It was furnished with two single beds, two desks, and a dresser. Andy was seated at his desk, proudly displaying a black and white photograph inside a frame. "Do you remember the man in this picture?" he asked.

"I sure do. It's a picture of Frank Mahovlich, my favorite hockey player."

Andy handed me the picture, and I showed it to the dogs.

"In the sixties," I said, "Frank Mahovlich played hockey for the Toronto Maple Leafs. He was one of their top scorers and helped them win four Stanley Cups. See the inscription on the bottom: 'To Claude: Best Wishes, Frank Mahovlich.' The picture was a birthday gift from my aunt. She had bought the picture at the team's arena. She also arranged for him to inscribe a personal message to me, and sign his name. Her gesture touched me. I cherished that picture for years."

"Most of the residents of our town were fans of the Montreal Canadiens. They wore the team's sweater, often with the number '9' on the back, in honor of Maurice Richard, one of hockey's greatest stars. He had been the first player in the National Hockey League to score fifty goals in one season, and the first player to score five hundred goals in a career."

But I was a fan of the Toronto Maple Leafs. My hero was Frank Mahovlich, and I wore his number '27' on my sweater. My friends often teased me, but my allegiance never wavered. It was well rewarded too. In the early sixties, the Maple Leafs were the best team in the league.

I handed the picture to Andy, who put it back on his desk, next to a stack of books.

"What are you studying?" I asked.

"Twelfth Night, a play by William Shakespeare." Then, he recited the first few lines of the play by heart:

"If music be the food of love, play on, Give me excess of it, that, surfeiting, The appetite may sicken and so die."

"That strain again: it had a dying fall…"

"Are you memorizing the play for a test?" asked Tommy.

Andy lowered his head, and said, "No. I got in trouble at school yesterday, and my punishment was memorizing the first page of the play by tomorrow morning."

"What did you do?"

"I broke a window at the school, but not on purpose. It was an accident."

"How did you break the window by accident?"

"During recess, my friends and I went to the schoolyard to practice our fielding. We were to take turns striking baseballs with a bat in the direction of the other boys who were to field them. But we couldn't find an empty spot, so we lingered in front of the school, a two-story building with a façade of large window panes for the classes, separated by thin columns of bricks. One of us dared the others to bat a baseball at the bricks without hitting the windows."

"I hope you refused," said Bobby.

"Not exactly. Another boy accepted the dare. He swung the bat with all his might but popped the baseball high in the air. It landed harmlessly on the roof. Breathing a sigh of relief, he handed the bat to another boy, who dithered and then handed the bat to me. I tried to hand the bat to other boys, but they declined. 'Somebody has to do this,' I said. I took a few practice swings, lobbed another ball in the air, and swung the bat on the sweet spot, sending the ball straight at the school."

"I hope you hit the bricks."

"Not exactly. I was close, very close. I only missed them by a few inches. The baseball crashed into a window, making a terrible noise. Everybody in the yard looked up and saw us running away. After recess, the school principal summoned us to her office. She asked us who had broken the window, and even though I kept my silence, my friends betrayed me. In my defense, I told the principal that I had broken the window by accident, but she just rolled her eyes. Clearly, she had already decided I was guilty, and was eager to punish me."

I could tell that the dogs were dismayed, but for some reason, their dismay was directed at me, not Andy. I tried to correct the record. Referring to myself in the third person, I said, "You must remember that Andy smashed the window, not Claude. Yes, technically, Andy and Claude are one and the same person, but there's a big difference in age between them. Andy was thirteen years old when he smashed the window, and Claude is sixty years old now, a difference of nearly fifty years. Claude would have never smashed a window. He's too mature, and responsible."

"Why is the age difference relevant?" asked Tommy.

"It allowed Andy to improve himself and become more responsible. I like to say that it allowed Andy to blossom into Claude, like a caterpillar blossoms into a butterfly."

"I guess you're saying that I'll still be a caterpillar when I'm thirteen years old."

"Yes. It took you a few years to blossom."

"I can see myself sitting at a desk in the library of a High School when I'm fifteen years old, studying for a Chemistry test. Will I be Andy the caterpillar or Claude the butterfly by then?"

"I do believe you're thinking of the time I was memorizing the principles of matter and energy for a Chemistry test. I think you were Claude by then."

Andy sneered. Facing Tommy and Bobby, he said, "Claude the butterfly will be in the library preparing for a Chemistry test, not by memorizing the principles of matter and energy, but by memorizing answers on a cheat sheet." The dogs frowned.

"That's right. When Claude is in high school, the same Chemistry course will be taught twice on the same day, once in the morning, and once in the afternoon. The instructor will teach the same lessons, and give the same tests in both classes."

"The tests will be multiple choice. The test papers will consist of questions accompanied by several possible answers, all of them wrong except one. Students will be asked to identify the correct answer for each question."

"Claude will have a friend, an excellent student, who will also take the same course. His friend will attend the morning class, and Claude will attend the afternoon class. The friend will take the test in the morning, and Claude will take it in the afternoon. When he takes his test, the friend will record the correct answers on a cheat sheet, and after the test, hand the cheat sheet to Claude."

"He owed me a favor," I said.

"On the cheat sheet, the friend will identify the correct answers to the questions. During the lunch period, Claude will go to the library and memorize the cheat sheet."

"But a classmate will catch Claude cheating in the library. He'll grab the cheat sheet from him, and run away before Claude is finished. Claude will leave the library, find himself a corner, and rack his brain to recall the correct answers. In class, as other students are writing the test, he'll still be racking their brains to recall the answers on the cheat sheet. When the period is nearly over, he'll give up, and guess the answers. Needless to say, he'll fail the test miserably."

"Maybe, but it was the last time I ever cheated on a test."

# Chapter 13

Andy was on a roll. "Now, I can see myself sitting next to my father at the kitchen table of my home. I'm seventeen years old, studying for an exam in Mathematics. Will I have blossomed into Claude the butterfly by then?"

"Yes, there's a good probability."

Again, Andy turned to the dogs. "Although Claude won't cheat on tests again, he will completely bungle two exams." I dropped my shoulders.

Andy said, "When he's in high school, Claude will lose interest in his education. He'll skip classes, arrive late, and doodle or daydream. He won't do homework, or study for exams. He'll loiter at a friend's house for hours, drinking coffee, smoking cigarettes, and listening to rock music. But he'll encourage his parents to think that, despite appearances, he is diligently applying himself to his studies."

"Just before the Christmas holiday, he'll be scheduled to write two exams: Math and Physics. Naturally, he'll know nothing about either subject."

Hoping to put an end to the drama, I interrupted Andy and continued the story. "But this time, I felt inspired to turn a new leaf and score well on the exam. My father had taught

Math in high school and in university, and when I was younger, he tutored me regularly. A few days before the Math exam, I asked him to explain the Pyromanian Theory to me. He wondered whether I meant the Pythagorean Theorem. To be on the safe side, I said, 'both.'"

"He suggested we start with the Pythagorean Theorem. I handed him my textbook. As he flipped the pages, he asked, 'Why do I suspect that this textbook has been sitting in the bottom of your locker all term?' I would have replied, 'Because the textbook has been sitting in the bottom of my locker all term,' but I knew that he knew."

"'When you have a right-angled triangle,' he said, 'the square of the hypotenuse is equal to the sum of the square of the two legs. A right-angled triangle is a triangle in which one of the three angles is equal to ninety degrees. The side opposite the right angle is called the hypotenuse. The two other sides are called the legs. Repeat what I just said.'"

"'You take your right-hand triangle, your square, your hypotenuse, and your two legs. You mix them all together, and voilà, you get the Pythagorean Theorem.' Chuckling, I watched my father rub his temples."

"'Please Dad,' I said, sheepishly, 'show me with examples.' He went to the end of the first chapter, read the first exercise aloud, and then solved it, explaining each step along the way. When he was finished, he asked me to solve the exercise by myself. I completed one or two steps, then stalled. He repeated the vexing step for me, then I completed it myself. I went on to complete a few more steps, until I stalled again, and waited for him to repeat the next vexing step. Back and forth we went until I managed to solve the first exercise alone. To ingrain the steps in me, he made me solve it twice more, from beginning to end. One by one, we completed all the exercises in the chapter. After a brief break, we tackled the exercises in the following chapter."

"Before long, I was learning and feeling smart. The more I learned, the more I wanted to learn. I even resolved to keep up with my studies in the future, instead of waiting till the last minute. After two long days of rigorous study, I solved the final exercise in the book and raised my arms in triumph. I knew the subject backward, and declared that I would ace the exam, maybe even get the top grade in the class."

"What grade did you get?" asked Tommy.

"I believe the top grade."

"I believe no grade at all," interjected Andy, who had been listening to me intently. On the morning of the exam, Claude will strut to school, take his seat inside the cafeteria, and wait impatiently for his 'MATHEMATICS EXAMINATION' paper. When the teacher hands Claude a paper, he'll snatch it as if it were a treat, but to his dismay, he'll read the title 'PHYSICS EXAMINATION' on the cover.

"Nervous, he'll tell the teacher, 'I must be in the wrong room. This is a Physics exam. I'm supposed to be writing the Math exam. Can you direct me to the right room?' The teacher will reply, 'You are in the right room. There is no Math exam anywhere in this school today. It was held two days ago. Today is the Physics exam.'"

"Feeling the wind knocked out of him, Claude will return to his seat, flip the pages of the exam paper, write his name on the cover, doodle around his name, put his pen on the desk, and bury his head in his arms during the entire exam. Not only will he abstain from writing the exam, but he'll also abstain from reading it. When the Physics exam is over, he'll just hand in his paper, blank but for his name and the doodles."

Andy saw that the dogs were eager to hear more stories. "You might think that Claude will feel very badly about failing both exams and wasting two days of his father's life. In fact, Claude will feel very bad, but not for very long. He'll recover his mood when he meets his friends outside the school. Some of them will have been exempted from writing exams due to good grades. The others will have finished writing their exams. All of them will be eager for Claude to finish his Physics exam in two days so they can go on a ski trip. But Claude will have a surprise for them. He'll suggest that they leave the next morning, claiming that the Physics exam has been postponed until the new year."

Thrilled, the boys will pack their skis and equipment in the car belonging to Claude's parents, who will have kindly agreed to lend it to Claude for the trip. Then, the boys will go to the ski hill by car.

"A funny thing will happen on the way to the ski hill."

"The sun will shine when they leave, but weather conditions will deteriorate on the way. It will rain, and the rain will freeze when it hits the ground. Claude will drive in the driving lane of a highway with two lanes, one in each direction. There will be no barrier between the lanes. He'll borrow the passing lane whenever he wants to pass other cars in his lane. Because of the slippery conditions, the other cars on the highway will be moving slowly, too slowly for

Claude. He'll decide to pass every car he meets in his lane. What better way to impress his friends."

I wanted to interrupt Andy, not because he was lying, but because he was being overly dramatic. Hoping to lower the tone a notch, I offered to take over, but Bobby stopped me. "Andy is doing just fine," he said.

"On the highway," resumed Andy, "Claude will catch up to a car in the driving lane, and complain that the driver has fallen asleep at the wheel. He'll borrow the passing lane, and pass the car without incident. He'll also pass the next car in his lane, and the next car. Although the car will slide once, he'll regain control by stepping off the gas pedal. Finally, he'll come upon a queue of three cars, and decide to pass them all in one go. He'll pass the third car. A dot will appear on the horizon. He'll speed up a little and pass the second car. The size of the dot will grow, and he'll realize that he's facing a transport truck in the passing lane. His friends will urge him to hurry. But the first two cars will be close to each other, and instead of squeezing between them, he'll speed up a lot."

"After passing the first car in the queue, Claude's car will drift sideways. It will slide across the driving lane, and the two right wheels will leave the pavement. He'll try to steer the car back on the pavement, but the car will not respond. He'll jerk the steering wheel left. The car will climb back on the pavement, but rotate left. He'll jerk the steering wheel right, and the car will rotate right. Soon, he'll lose all control. No matter which way he turns the steering wheel, the car will just slide backward. Feeling helpless, he'll stare at his rearview mirror, and brace himself for a collision with the transport truck. His life will flash before his eyes."

"Lo and behold, an invisible hand will push the car off the passing lane, and off the driving lane. The car will slide backward along the shoulder till it slams into a snowbank, trunk first. The transport truck will roll past the car, blaring its horn. For a few seconds, the boys will sit frozen in the car, grateful to be alive."

"Shaking, Claude will step outside, walk to the back of the car, and inspect the damage. The exhaust pipe will be bent and the gasoline tank will be crooked, but the other parts will seem to be intact. After he and his friends dislodge the car from the snowbank, he'll turn it around, and finish the drive at a snail's pace. One by one, the cars he has passed will pass him."

"During the ski trip," said Andy, "Claude will forget all about his exams, but when he returns home and receives his report card, he'll have to face his father."

"May I interrupt," I said. "My report card was horrible. I received no grade in either Math or Physics and failed the other subjects. I was very remorseful. When I told my father, I apologized."

"He reminded me of the George Washington story, and forgave me."

"What is the George Washington story?" asked Bobby.

"When George Washington was a boy, he received a hatchet as a gift and chopped down a cherry tree in his father's garden. When his father confronted him, George said, 'Father, I cannot tell a lie, I did chop down the tree.' His father embraced him and forgave him. I had a similar moment with my father. When he saw my grades, he asked me if the report card was mine. I replied, 'Father, I cannot tell a lie. It is mine, and the grades are mine too.' He was so impressed with my candor that he embraced and forgave me. End of story."

Bobby turned to Andy, and said, "Claude is no George Washington. What did he really tell his father?"

"If you must know," said Andy, "Claude will alter the grades on his report card, leaving the impression that he has obtained excellent grades. When he sees the report card, his father will seem satisfied, but when he flips the card, he'll see that the teachers' comments do not match the grades. For example, the comment from the Match teacher will be, 'Claude forgot to write the exam.' And the comment from the Physics teacher will be, 'Claude doodled during the whole exam.' His father will infer that someone has altered the grades."

"I know the ending," said Bobby. "When his father asked for an explanation, Claude told him that he could not tell a lie and that John had altered the grades."

Andy guffawed, and said, "No. His father won't ask for an explanation. He'll just order him to go to his bedroom to contemplate his imminent punishment."

"I hope he got a good spanking," said Bobby.

"His father will go to the kitchen to get a wooden spoon, one used primarily to mix liquids in cooking, like soup and gravy but also used effectively to discipline bad boys. When he goes to his bedroom, Claude will shut the door and press his ear against it. He'll hear his father open a drawer, and jiggle the utensils. After a few minutes, His father will ask him if he knows where the wooden spoon is. Of course, Claude will know. The wooden spoon will be lying on the floor behind the stove where he put it, and all the other wooden spoons in the kitchen. Instead, he'll mislead his father by suggesting he look inside the cupboards and the drawers. A few minutes later, his father will announce that he has found the wooden spoon and that Claude can expect a visit from him soon."

After a pause, Bobby said, "Don't stop now."

Andy shook his head and said, "His father will not go to Claude's bedroom. He'll go back to the den while Claude withers in his bedroom, agonizing about a spanking that will never come."

"An hour later, Claude will leave the bedroom, creep into the den, and sit next to his father, who will put an arm around him to show that all is forgiven."

# Chapter 14

We left Andy's bedroom and climbed the stairs to the kitchen, a small but tidy room. We saw a sink, counters, and cupboards against one wall, a small stove and refrigerator against another wall, and a table surrounded by five chairs in the middle of the room. "The booster chair is for my brother Luc," I told the dogs, "and the high chair is for my brother Pierre."

A woman and a man stood at the sink, their backs turned to us. She was washing dishes, and he was drying them.

Andy walked up to his parents, and said, "I finished my homework. May I go see Pierre and Luc with my friends?"

"Who are your friends?" asked the man.

"Claude, Tommy, and Bobby."

"Who is Claude?"

"He's me when I'm sixty years old."

His parents looked at each other. The man asked, "And who are Tommy and Bobby?"

"They're Claude's dogs."

The man turned around. He had a handsome face and thinning hair. He wore dress pants, slippers, and a white shirt with long sleeves that had been rolled up to the elbows.

"Are you sure your friends are with you?" he asked. "I think you forgot them downstairs."

"No, they're with me."

"What do you think, Mom?" asked the man.

She looked over her shoulder, and said, "I can hear Pierre whimpering. See if his diaper is soiled. But Luc just fell asleep. I don't want him to be disturbed. Stay out of his bedroom."

Andy led us down the hall. There were two bedrooms. He shut the door of Luc's bedroom, then stepped into the master bedroom. A double bed filled most of the space. There were two dressers against a wall and a crib against another. Cotton cloth diapers were folded neatly on a small table beside the crib.

"Meet Pierre," said Andy. The dogs and I looked inside the crib and cooed over a baby who was fidgeting uncomfortably. "I need to change his diaper," he added. Bobby sniffed the diaper and gagged.

"The smell can't be that bad," I told him. "I've been picking up your stools all your life. I'm still alive."

"How should I know?" asked Bobby. "I've never had to pick up your stools."

Andy pulled down Pierre's plastic underpants, undid a pin on the soiled diaper, and threw the diaper inside a pail, but not before a pungent smell of ammonia nearly made him heave. He took a clean diaper, and holding two points, folded it to form a triangle. He lifted Pierre by the ankles, washed his bum with a wet cloth, and slipped the clean diaper under the bum. He joined three points over Pierre's belly and attached the points with a pin. Finally, he slipped the plastic underpants over the clean diaper and exhaled.

I turned to face the dogs, and said, “In those days, babies wore cloth diapers, and when the diapers were soiled, we washed them. We didn’t throw them away.”

Andy turned to face us, and asked, “Why should we throw away dirty diapers? We don’t throw away dirty clothes.”

I nodded, and said, “When Pierre is a little older but still wearing diapers, you’ll play a game of cat and mouse with him. When you see him, you’ll pinch your nose, and accuse him of soiling his diaper. When Pierre shakes his head, you’ll demand to smell it. Pierre will run away. You’ll chase him from room to room, but you’ll never catch him. Even when you corner him, you’ll let him escape.”

“Pierre started fidgeting again. Gazing at him lovingly, Andy brushed his hair with his fingers, and whispered softly, ‘You’re just a tiny baby today. All you do is sleep, drink, and poop. Sleep, drink, and poop. But one day, you’ll walk, play, and work. You’ll make friends, go to school, get a job, meet a girl, get married, and have children. You and I will live close to each other, and visit each other regularly.’”

Pierre fell asleep.

“What a beautiful boy,” said Andy. “He’s so lovable.”

“Except a few years later,” I said, “he became very unruly. One night, Mom and Dad asked John and me to babysit him while they went out together. Before leaving, they instructed us to put him to bed at eight o’clock.”

“We watched television in the living room. When it was time, I carried him into the bedroom and tucked him under the blankets, but he squeezed my neck and refused to let go.”

“I went back into the living room with Pierre hanging from my neck. Hoping to sap his energy, I encouraged him to jump up and down on the couch. At one point, he sat down, his eyelids drooped, and his head tilted down. Thinking he was asleep, I carried him into the bedroom. I laid him on the bed and pulled the blankets over him, but as soon as I left the bedroom, he pushed the blankets away, giggled, stood up, and started jumping on the mattress.”

“I put him to bed a third time, and begged him to go to sleep, but he kept finding excuses to stay up. He wanted me to lie beside him. He wanted me to get him a glass of water. He wanted me to play a game with him. He wanted me to read him a story. He wanted me to take him to the bathroom. Feigning anger, I refused and stomped out of the room. For a few seconds, the room fell silent. Then, I heard him standing behind the door, calling my name.”

“Exasperated, John and I walked to the next house, and rang the doorbell. Looking very groggy, our neighbor answered the door in her nightgown. We asked her to help us put Pierre to sleep. She followed us to our house, but when she entered the bedroom, she found Pierre fast asleep in the bed. She waited a few seconds, checked on him, shrugged her shoulders, bade us good night, and left the house. John and I were thoroughly embarrassed.” Andy frowned.

“What was Pierre like?” asked Tommy.

“Pierre was very congenial. The family moved to a new house when he was six years old. He went to the surrounding houses and introduced himself to the neighbors.”

"He was also one of the most decisive persons I ever knew. When he made up his mind about something, anything, nobody could change it. When he set a task for himself, he saw it through to the end. All his life, he worked in the restaurant industry, first as a fast food worker, then as a franchise owner, and finally as a senior executive in charge of opening franchise stores in different cities, a position he still holds today."

"He also met his future wife in high school, when both were only fourteen years old. I remember spying on them when I first heard the rumor of a relationship. At lunchtime, I went to their school and saw them sharing lunch at a table in the cafeteria, oblivious to the students around them. Knowing how jealous Pierre was of his dignity, I left without getting caught. Little did I know that they would eventually marry, and have three children. They were a perfect couple. I never saw them argue."

"Come to think of it, my brother John was also happily married. I never saw him and his wife argue either. I never argued with my wife, but only because I was single my entire life."

"Two funny stories about Pierre come to mind. Once, when he was only seven years old, he was playing a hockey game. He slipped behind the opposing defensemen, received a pass from a teammate, and skated toward the net on a breakaway. But his skates were too big. One of them flew off his foot and slid down the ice. He fell but got up, and hobbled toward the net on one skate, still intent on scoring, but the puck was stolen from him before he could shoot."

"Also, when Pierre was learning to ski, my parents bought him ski boots so big that he could slip in and out of them without adjusting the buckles. At the end of the day, when it was time to go home, my mother just stepped on his skis and lifted him by the armpits. She carried him to the car while I followed them with his equipment. There was no risk of injury. He skied on a baby hill that was almost flat."

# Chapter 15

We were still in the master bedroom, taking turns rocking Pierre's crib.

"Did you have other dogs before us?" asked Tommy.

"No. You were my first dog, and Bobby was my second. I was afraid of dogs for many years because I was attacked by one when I was a boy."

"I'm sure you provoked the dog," said Bobby.

"No. There was a pause. 'My parents wanted their children to be fluent in both French and English. But in our town, most residents were francophone. So, for years, they sent us to a summer camp to make friends with boys who spoke English."

"The camp was in a field near a river and contained various cabins, including a cafeteria, a chapel, a workshop, and sleeping quarters. On the river, there were docks, canoes, diving towers, and a string of flags enclosing the swimming area."

"I remember my first stay at the camp. I was very nervous about leaving my family and friends and living among strangers who spoke a language I barely understood."

“One summer, there was a dog at the camp. It often sat next to the door of the cafeteria. After lunch one day, a supervisor told us that we would be spending the afternoon at the workshop to learn arts and crafts. We cheered, bolted out of the cafeteria, and raced across the field to arrive first at the workshop. The dog noticed us and gave chase. I thought it would just run alongside us. I heard it barking in the background, but I was too busy racing to pay attention. Suddenly, I felt a heavy object land on my back. I stumbled but tried to keep running. Then, the dog bit me on the shoulder, the side, and the buttocks, drawing blood.”

“My brother John came to my aid. He walked me to the infirmary, where a supervisor put bandages on my wounds, and drove me to the hospital. When I was discharged a week later, I returned to the camp. The dog was gone, and I wondered what had happened to it. I asked other campers, but none of them knew.”

“I know what happened,” said Bobby. “After it bit you, the dog got rabies.”

We all harbor a fear that is so deeply ingrained, it haunts us continuously. We resign ourselves to it and learn to live with it, even when we see other people who are impervious to it. One day, we hide the fear to overcome a crisis. Then, we wonder how the fear could possibly control us for so long, and we banish it forever. Mine was a fear of dogs, which haunted me until the day I confronted a Doberman Pinscher in my late teens.

“Behind our house, there was a small park with benches and swings. On weekdays, mothers brought their children to play on the swings. On weekends, high school students sat on the benches to drink beer. Sunday mornings, my father went to the park, collected the empty beer bottles, and redeemed them at a beer store."

"I was asleep in my bed when my mother burst into the room, yelling, 'A dog is attacking your father in the park. Go help him.' I jumped out of bed, grabbed the first object I saw, my tennis racket, and ran out of the back of the house. A Doberman Pinscher was barking aggressively at my father, who was standing on a bench, hunched over, and pointing an empty beer bottle at it. My father had just been released from hospital after surgery. The scar on his side was fresh and sensitive."

"I yelled at the dog, and threw my tennis racket at it."

"Did the racket hit your father?" asked Bobby.

"No, of course not, but it also missed the dog. Surprised, the dog looked up at me and then fled across the field. I pursued it to the other side of the park, where it stopped, lowered its head, and looked at me with sad eyes. I was in no mood to forgive. I waved my arms and yelled at the top of my lungs. I swear that dog just turned around and hurried behind the high school, its tail between its legs."

"I never saw the dog near the park again." I heard Andy sigh.

"What is it now?" I asked.

Turning to the dogs, he said, "After Claude throws the tennis racket, the Doberman Pinscher will take the tennis racket in its teeth, and lure Claude to the end of the park, then drop the racket. As Claude retrieves the racket, the dog will run back to the house. His father will try to shuffle home, but the dog will gain on him. At the last minute, the back door will swing open and Claude's mother will jump outside, and chase the dog away. That's when the dog will escape behind the high school."

"That's what I said."

"I think not," said Bobby.

"Anyway, my point is that I lost my fear of dogs that day."

Fibbing is one thing. If we get caught, we know we'll lose credibility. But if we tell a story we believe to be true, but it's false, we're not lying. We should be forgiven, unless, of course, we were caught fibbing in the past, in which case, we need someone else to corroborate our story.

I turned to face Bobby, and said, "Wait till you hear my next story. Tommy, I'll ask you to confirm it because you were there also. Do you remember the time we were walking along a road, and I saved you from the wolf?"

Tommy frowned and asked politely, "Are you sure I was there?"

I should have taken the hint. Instead, I replied, "How could you forget? We were walking down an old road in a municipal park. The road was closed to motor vehicles, but open to pedestrians and cyclists. It cut through woods and fields but led nowhere. At the end of the road, we turned around and backtracked to the parking lot."

"I remember the road," said Tommy, "but not the wolf."

Another hint ignored. "Early one morning, you and I went for a walk down the road. I untied your leash, and you walked beside me. As we approached the end of the road, I turned around and saw a wolf stalking us, its head and tail held high. Shivers ran down my spine. I quickly tied the leash to your collar, then grabbed a broken branch, and removed its twigs to make a shaft that would be stiff enough to sting a wolf. I looked again. The wolf was close, and getting closer."

"When we reached the end of the road, you and I turned around. You noticed the wolf for the first time and started barking. With one hand, I held you by the leash, and with the other, I swung the staff at the wolf. It hesitated, then fled into the woods. Now, do you remember?"

"I do remember," replied Tommy, "but your wolf was just a big dog trying to befriend us."

# Chapter 16

"Maybe we should talk about something else," said Tommy.

"Claude, were you ever married?" I shook my head.

"Did you ever have children?"

"No. I wanted children all my life. I dreamed of having them, guiding them, educating them, and playing with them. But you and Bobby came along. You were more than I could handle." The dogs scoffed.

"But I was very close to my nephews and nieces and even participated in their upbringings. You know, an old uncle acquires a lot of wisdom from a lifetime of trials and tribulations and is anxious to dispense his wisdom to the next generation to spare the pain and humiliation that he himself had to endure. The last thing he wants is to take this wisdom with him to the grave. I've been dispensing my wisdom to my nephews and nieces for years. I like to think that I've been a good influence on them."

Andy interrupted me. "Tell Tommy and Bobby about the good influence you'll be on Michel when you take him to Parliament Hill."

Glaring at Andy, I said, "There's nothing to tell, really. Michel is my brother John's only son. When Michel was two years old, I took him to Parliament Hill, hoping to teach him to say the word 'Parliament'. It was my first time alone with him. When we arrived, I took him in my arms. He was awestruck by the majesty of the three buildings facing him: the West Block, the Centre Block, and the East Block. Pointing at the Centre Block, I said, 'Michel, the building in the middle with the big tower is named Parliament. Say Parliament.'"

"But Michel said, 'Castle.'"

I smiled. Obviously, an innocent child would think that the Centre Block was a castle. Built with thousands of stones in the Gothic style, it featured vertical bays, windows with pointed arches, intricate stone carvings, a copper roof, dormer windows, and last but not least, the Peace Tower. Nevertheless, I was determined to make him understand that this castle had a name.

"Can you say 'Parliament' for me?" I asked.

"'Castle,' he repeated, giggling."

"After a half hour of requests denied, I admitted defeat. We strolled along the grounds for the rest of the afternoon, then went home. I was unable to teach him to say 'Parliament'. Big deal."

"Actually," said Andy, "it will be a big deal to your brother because you'll teach Michel to swear. On the way home, a news item on the car radio will irritate you, and forgetting the presence of an impressionable young mind beside you, you'll curse the radio. Can you remember your exact words?"

"No, I forget."

"Your exact words will be 'fock off'. Right away, you'll hear an echo. 'Fock off,' Michel will say, imitating your voice, and capturing your emotion. He'll notice your jaw drop, and laugh. You'll try to correct him by substituting other phrases, but none of them will stick."

"How sad," said Bobby. "Two seconds was enough time for Claude to teach Michel to swear, but half an hour was too little time for him to teach Michel the name of a venerable institution."

"When you arrive at John's house, you'll open the front door, push Michel inside, ring the doorbell, and run back to your car. When John answers the door, he'll wave you inside, but you'll point at your wrist, pretending to be late for an appointment and drive away. John will call you at home, and ask if you taught his son to swear. As usual, you'll deny responsibility and then blame his classmates. John will remind you Michel is too young to go to school."

# Chapter 17

Bobby drew a heavy sigh, and said, "I hope you can find a better example of your good influence."

"I have a library brimming with stories," I said defiantly. "Let me start with Julie, Pierre's only daughter. She was smart, athletic, and excelled at school and sports. I often babysat her. I drew coloring books with her. I helped her with her homework. I took her places. The list goes on and on."

"You took her places like the village fair," said Andy, who turned to face the dogs, then declared, "You'll really like this story. Go ahead, Claude. Tell us. We're listening."

After a moment's hesitation, I began, "Pierre lived in a village that hosted a small fair at the end of the summer. He let me take Julie, his precious little girl, to the fair, even though she was only eight years old. She and I spent the afternoon walking around the fairground, admiring the games, the booths, and the rides. There was one ride that seemed to mesmerize her: the spinning tea cups."

"What are spinning teacups?" asked Tommy.

"People sit inside large tea cups, which spin on an axis and roll along a track. The faster the cups roll, the faster they spin." With my hand, I simulated the spinning motion of a cup rolling around a track. "'Do you want to go on the ride?' I asked Julie."

"She was reluctant. Her mood shifted between riding and watching. 'I'm not sure,' she said. 'It looks so scary.'"

"Trying to reassure her, I said, 'When I was a boy, the tea cups were my favorite ride. When the cup spins, it tickles your tummy. Why don't we go together?' Julie smiled and nodded."

"We waited in line, walked on the platform, and sat inside one of the tea cups. An attendant locked a security bar over our laps. I turned to Julie, smiled, and raised my shoulders in anticipation."

"The attendant pulled a lever, and the tea cups started to roll around the track. Julie started laughing, but I started feeling ill. My head was spinning, and my stomach was swirling. I took deep breaths, but my discomfort grew. After one revolution around the track, I was ready to hurl myself out of the teacup. After two revolutions, my last meal was ready to hurl itself out of my stomach. There were people standing on the perimeter of the ride watching the riders, and I imagined myself spraying them all. I tried to warn the attendant when we rolled past him. 'Stop,' I pleaded, but my plea fell on deaf ears. I screamed again the next time around, but Julie covered my mouth with her hand to muffle my screams. She was having too much fun."

"I leaned my head against the back of the cup, shut my eyes, held my breath, and counted numbers. 'Hold it for one more spin,' I repeated to myself, 'just one more spin.' It was no use. I felt a lump in my throat and braced myself for the imminent eruption. I pulled my shirt over my mouth, hoping to contain the mess. Suddenly, the attendant pulled the lever, and the rolling and spinning subsided. Seconds later, the tea cups came to a full stop. I still felt awful, but well enough to stand, step off the ride, and go home with Julie."

"But you skipped the best part," said Andy. Turning to the dogs, he said, "When the ride is over, Claude will stagger down the platform, shuffle between two tents, and collapse. Julie will stay with him for a while, then leave to seek help. Fortunately, she'll meet her father on the fairground who will come to Claude's aid."

# Chapter 18

"I wish I could tell you better stories," said Andy.

"And I wish you tried a little harder," I retorted.

"Richard is Pierre's younger son. I have two stories about him. One is bad, and the other is worse."

"Start with the bad one," said Bobby.

Assuming a somber expression, Andy said, "When Richard is five years old, Claude will take him rollerblading on the street. Before leaving the house, Pierre will tell him to put protective gloves on Richard's hands, in case he falls. When Claude reaches for the gloves on the floor of the closet, Richard will look at him, and shake his head. 'I don't need gloves,' he'll whisper. 'I won't fall.' Claude will grin, wink, and throw the gloves back on the floor. Off they will go on the street. At first, Richard will skate at a leisurely pace beside Claude, and Claude will watch up and down the street for cars. Then, Claude will run down the street, and spur Richard on. To please his uncle, Richard will skate faster. When Richard catches up to him, Claude will sprint down the street, leaving Richard behind again. Running backward, he'll incite Richard to skate even faster. Richard will try, but after a few strides, he'll trip on pebbles, fall on the pavement, and hurt himself. His little hands will be covered in scratches oozing blood. Richard will start to cry."

"Claude will carry Richard home in his arms, and try to comfort him by kissing his hands all better. At the house, Pierre will notice the blood on Richard's hands, and the gloves on the floor. The scowl on Pierre's face will convince Claude that he has overstayed his welcome."

"How can the other incident be worse?" asked Bobby.

"You be the judge," said Andy. Turning to me, he added, "Do stop me if I stray from the truth." I forced a smile.

Turning to the dogs, he resumed, "When Richard is twelve years old, he'll take up snowboarding. Aware of Richard's penchant for speed, Pierre will ask Claude to supervise him on the hill. Claude will accept."

"One night, Richard and Claude will ride up and down the ski hill together, Richard on his snowboard, and Claude on his skis. Richard will lead, Claude will follow, and Richard will never leave Claude's sight. But on the last run, Richard will pull ahead. He'll jump off the crest of a hill, and disappear under the crest. Claude will also jump off the crest. He'll see Richard parked on the hill below him, and when he lands, swerve sharply to avoid a collision. 'That was a close call,' he'll say. 'Richard, you're standing on the wrong side of the hill. People coming over the crest cannot see you. They'll crash into you unless you move. Follow me to the other side.' Claude will traverse the hill, and urge Richard to join him, but Richard will shake his head, and stay put. Then, as predicted, a snowboarder will fly over the crest, and crash into him. Into Richard? asked Tommy."

"No, no, no. The snowboarder will crash into the back of Claude's knees, causing him to flip backward, and land heavily on his head. Stunned, Claude will lie motionless on the hill to assess his injuries. Richard will rush over, make sure the injuries are minor, then retrieve Claude's skis, poles, toque, and goggles, scattered down the hill. Adding insult to injury, the snowboarder will berate Claude for stopping on the wrong side of the hill."

"But these were isolated mishaps," I said. "Overall, I was a good influence. I can recall the time I helped Dan, Pierre's older son, complete an essay on a famous explorer of the sixteenth century. Dan was supposed to read a chapter in a book and then summarize the important points in his own words. But at home, he was finding it hard to focus on his project. There were too many distractions. The deadline was looming."

"I brought him to my office, where he was exposed to silence and inspiration. In less than two hours of concentrated effort, he was finished. I browsed through his essay and was impressed with his effort. I typed the essay for him, gave it a scholarly look, and handed it to him. If memory serves, he received an excellent grade."

"Your memory is doing you a real disservice," said Andy. "Dan will receive an excellent grade for another essay he has to write."

"Yes, you'll type Dan's paper, but thinking that it has spelling and grammatical mistakes, you'll make unauthorized corrections before you hand him the paper."

"Weeks will pass without news, and the suspense will gnaw at you. Unable to wait any longer, you'll call Pierre for an update. Never one to mince words, he'll say, 'You almost had Dan expelled from school. The teacher called him into her office to review spelling and grammatical mistakes in his essay, and to express her suspicion that someone else had tampered with it. Dan scanned the essay and confirmed her suspicions, but refused to snitch on you. Fortunately, she believed him and asked him to write a second essay. Dan complied, and received an excellent grade for the second essay, not the first.'"

# Chapter 19

"Let me see," said Bobby, "You taught Michel to swear; you lost Julie at a crowded fair; you exposed Richard to injury on a ski hill; and you butchered Dan's essay. I can see why your brothers decided to restrict your access to their children."

"Frankly, I'm losing hope. But Claude, I'm a generous dog. I'll give you one more chance to redeem yourself. Cite me one good deed that you did, just one."

"I can cite many deeds involving my mother," I claimed.

"Sure. How well you treat your mother is all I need to know about how well you treat other people."

"All my life, I was a dutiful son. There are so many examples. I hardly know where to begin."

"Go to your library brimming with stories," said Andy. "You'll find one of your mother's visits to your new house."

Scowling at Andy, I began, "I had just bought a new house when Mom came to visit me. She was elderly by then. I was hoping to convince her to sell her own house and move into mine. Living alone was becoming a challenge for her."

“My house was a bungalow with a façade made of red brick. The garage was on the left and protruded toward the street. The living room was on the right and set further back. The front entrance was in the middle. When she arrived, I led her through a short corridor to a large open space that served as a den and a dining room. The den was furnished with a table, sofa, and reclining leather chair. I said ‘Mom, this den will be your private space. The dogs will never bother you there.’”

“Another corridor led to the other side of the house. At the end of it, there were two bedrooms, a smaller bedroom on the left for me, and the master bedroom on the right, which I had adapted for her comfort. It contained a bed, a dresser, a television set, and two night tables. ‘This is your bedroom,’ I said. ‘You’ll be able to knit, read, and watch television from your bed, all alone. Behind that door is your bathroom, complete with a bathtub. Now, take a few minutes to unpack your things, then come join me in the den.’”

Mom reminded me that dogs made her nervous, but I reassured her that my playpen would keep her safe from my dogs.

“A few minutes later, Mom came to the den and began to read in her chair. The dogs were in the backyard. When they saw her profile in the window, they barked to come inside. I unfolded the playpen and opened a sliding door. The dogs ran inside the house to meet her, but the playpen performed admirably. It separated the dogs from Mom, as I had promised. She spent a wonderful weekend at my house.”

"Except," said Andy, "when Claude retrieves the playpen, he'll unfold it around his mother's chair. Can you believe it? The playpen will enclose his mother, not the dogs."

"I see," said Bobby. "Instead of preventing the dogs from jumping on Claude's mother, the playpen prevented his mother from jumping on the dogs."

"Exactly. When the dogs enter the house, they'll roam around the playpen. Claude will boast, 'See how safe you are inside your playpen.'"

"Naturally, his mother will suggest that a playpen should be used to confine his dogs, not his mother. But Claude will remind her that there are two of them, but only one of her."

"If only words could be retracted," said Bobby, adding, "I think I can see the ending. Claude's mother called her other sons, and begged them to rescue her from the playpen."

"I'm sure she'll think of it," said Andy "But, in fact, she'll spend the entire weekend isolated in her bedroom. Claude will hardly see her. She might as well have stayed in her own home."

Angry and embarrassed, I told Bobby, "Look who's talking, as if your treatment of my mother was any better. I'm thinking of the night that you stole her doggie bag. She had made reservations for the entire family at an Italian restaurant. It was our last family outing before her trip to Florida. Mom and I joined John and Pierre, and their families at a restaurant. She ordered a plate of spaghetti, which she couldn't finish, and put the leftovers in a doggie bag for future consumption."

“In the car, she slid the container under her seat. The car was a hatchback with a seat in the front and a cargo space in the back. Mom and I sat in the front seat. You and Tommy sat in the cargo space. I had installed a metal partition between the front and the cargo space that was nearly as wide as the interior. It should have confined you to the cargo space.”

“After dinner, my mother and I drove to a coffee shop to buy two cups of coffee to take home. We were only gone a few minutes. Imagine our surprise when we returned to the car, and saw you sitting in the front seat. I put you back in the cargo space.”

“‘Claude,’ said my mother, ‘my spaghetti is gone. I think Bobby ate it.’ She handed me the empty container.”

“I turned around and looked at the dogs. ‘Who ate the spaghetti?’ I asked. Your muzzle was all red. You were still licking the tomato sauce on your face. A strand of spaghetti was hanging from your mouth.”

“I cannot tell a lie,” said Bobby, “Tommy ate the spaghetti.” There was a moment of silence. “All right, I ate it. But it was a special spaghetti, covered in a rich sauce of ripe tomatoes and ground beef, sautéed with fresh onions, celery, and garlic, and seasoned with herbs and spices. The aroma in the car was killing me. I couldn’t help myself.”

I wasn’t finished. “And do you remember the slice of pizza you stole from her?”

“I stole it from you.”

“Yes, but I had bought it for her. It was the night I stopped at a local pizzeria to buy the slice. When I returned to the car, I saw your eyes fixated on the slice, so I was careful. I put the slice on the dashboard, and drove home, holding the steering wheel with one hand, and your collar with the other hand."

"When we arrived home, I held the plate high above my head, like a waiter holding a tray in a crowded room."

"You squatted. To my utter, utter dismay, you jumped and poked the back of my hand. 'Noooo…' I moaned, watching my pizza slice spiraling in the air toward the floor. You snatched it just before the floor was splattered with double cheese, extra pepperoni, jalapenos, pineapple, and mushrooms. You chewed it a few times, then sent it down the hatch."

"I expected you to be sick that night. But you burped, curled yourself in a ball on the floor, and slept comfortably all night."

# Chapter 20

We were still gazing at Pierre in his crib when Andy's father entered the master bedroom, and asked Andy, "Are your friends still with you?"

"Yes."

"Please ask them to go home. You should pack your suitcase before we leave."

"Sure, Dad." His father left the bedroom.

Andy said, "It won't take me long to pack. Do you want to meet again in an hour?"

"Sure, if there's enough time. Where?"

"At the boulder in the park."

I nodded, and said, "Meantime, I'll take the dogs for a walk. I'll show them the route that Dad followed on his walks."

Andy smiled. Tommy, Bobby, and I left the house.

"Every night after dinner," I said, "my father walked along the same route around town."

"How old were you when you started to go on walks with him?" asked Tommy.

"I think about six years old. We walked side by side. He only held my hand to avoid a hazard. Sometimes, we walked alone, and sometimes John or my mother accompanied us."

The dogs and I walked past the arena, the railroad tracks, and a convenience store, then came upon a three-story building made of red brick with a bay in the middle. "This is a hospital," I said.

"What is a hospital?" asked Tommy.

"It's an animal clinic for people. When I was seven years old, I had my tonsils removed at this hospital. My room was on the second floor. Before the operation, the doctor covered my face with a rubber mask that released ether, a gas that put me to sleep. The ether had a sweet but unpleasant smell. I cried until I lost consciousness."

"The smell of ether haunted me for years. Some scents in everyday life reminded me of it and made me shiver. Nowadays, ether is rarely used because it's highly flammable. When he came for a visit, my father asked the doctor if I had cried before the operation. The doctor said no. I was grateful to him for being more sensitive than truthful."

We turned at an intersection. The street was a busy artery leading to the commercial center of town. Kids on muscle bikes, fitted with monkey bars, banana seats, and console shifters raced past us on the sidewalk without seeing us.

We came upon a motel, and I said, "My friend's father owned this motel. They lived in a house on my street."

We were now walking along the main street of town. Pedestrians ambled along the sidewalks, stood at the storefronts, and shopped inside the stores. I said, "We'll be coming to a coffee shop soon, which baked the best doughnuts I ever tasted. I can see the sign from here. My father and I stopped at the shop to buy doughnuts for the rest of the walk home."

"Once, when Mom came with us on a walk, Dad tried to bypass the shop. He was trying to conceal our patronage of it. At the time, he was following a strict diet to lose weight, and doughnuts were not included in the diet. Doughnuts, however, were very much included in mine."

When I saw the coffee shop, I started to skip in anticipation, grabbed his hand, and pointed at the shop. Normally, Dad shared my enthusiasm, but this time, he feigned indifference. As we neared the shop, I dug my heels in the sidewalk, and went limp, causing him to stumble. 'What's wrong?' asked Mom. 'Doughnuts,' I said. 'We forgot to stop for doughnuts.' She looked at Dad, and asked, 'Have you been coming here for doughnuts all this time?' My father shook his head unconvincingly.

"She hesitated, then said, 'In that case, you won't mind if Claude and I buy ourselves one doughnut each.' Dad tried to follow us inside the shop, but she stopped him at the door. 'Wait for us here. We won't be long.'"

"I described the various flavors to her. She bought a maple doughnut for herself, and a strawberry doughnut for me. We savored the doughnuts on the rest of the walk, as my father watched with envy. I felt bad for him, but not bad enough to help him break his diet."

The dogs and I turned into another street and stopped at a two-story building with a façade of dull grey stone veneer. On the first floor, there was a row of retail shops, each with an entrance and a storefront window displaying wares for sale. On the second floor, there was a row of office windows.

"My father worked on the second floor," I said. "He had an office with two rooms, each with a desk. One weekend, he took me to the office. He spent his time in one room shuffling papers and moving boxes, while I sat at his desk in the other room, spinning in his swivel chair. On the desk, I saw an ink pad, a stamp engraved with his signature, and a stack of letters. Thinking I was doing him a favor, I pressed the stamp on the pad, then I pressed it above his name on each letter, being careful not to smudge the ink. When I was finished, I placed the stamped letters neatly on his secretary's desk. He never noticed my handiwork."

"Neither did his secretary. She had typed the letters and left them on his desk for his review over the weekend. On Monday morning, when she arrived at work, she saw the stamped letters on her desk and mailed them."

"One of the letters was addressed to his boss. A few days later, he called my father to tease him about spelling mistakes in his letter and jocularly offered to edit his letters in the future. Although Dad was puzzled at first because he couldn't recall signing the letter, he quickly realized who the culprit was."

"The incident should have embarrassed him. As a school inspector, he assessed the language proficiency of the teachers under his supervision. His boss had received a letter with elementary mistakes suggesting that Dad's own proficiency was wanting. Still, he never admonished me. I never knew about it until my mother told me years later."

Next, we stopped in front of an imposing building made of bricks and large window panes. I said, "I attended this school for six years. Mostly, we walked or rode our bikes to school. In bad weather, our parents drove us to school. I never rode in a bus to school."

"Dad's route around town was a loop. The hospital we just saw is down this street. You can see it in the distance."

"How old were you when you began walking to school?"

"Five years old. We walked alone or with our classmates. Walking to school was common then. The round trip between my home and the school was one hour. One afternoon, when I was in the first grade, I walked between home and school three times. When the bell rang for recess, I thought it was the end of the day and left the school. When I arrived home, my mother was waiting for me. I think the teacher had alerted her by telephone. She told me I was early, and asked me to keep busy until dinner. But all my friends were still in school, and I got bored. So, I decided to leave home. When I arrived at school, I heard another bell. It was now the end of the day and time to leave the school. I met my friends at the door, and we walked home together. My mother was more amused than alarmed."

"As soon as I received my first bicycle, I was allowed to ride it to school. My first cycle was a tricycle, which had one wheel in the front, and two wheels in the back. I taught myself to ride on two wheels by leaning on one side, causing the back wheel on the other side to lift, and rolling along the street on the other two wheels. It was a bit like doing a wheelie on a bicycle."

"One day, I asked my mother to look out the kitchen window to watch my new trick. I ran outside, hopped on my tricycle, and, making sure she was still looking, weaved my way down the street on two wheels. She rushed outside and grabbed the handlebars to stop me. But she must have told my father that I had outgrown the tricycle. A few days later, they bought me a brand-new bicycle. It was too big for me at first. My feet could barely reach the pedals at the bottom of the chain ring. But I enjoyed riding it, and in time, grew into it."

The dogs and I walked along the side of the building. "What is that contraption?" asked Bobby, pointing at a narrow steel staircase running down the side of the building, from the third floor to the ground.

"It was an emergency fire escape," I said, "in case the school caught fire. If the halls were filled with smoke, the pupils could escape by going down the fire escape."

"It looks very steep," said Tommy.

I nodded, and said, "It looks even steeper from the top. We held practice drills once or twice a year. When the alarm sounded, we left the classroom, opened the doors, and stepped down the fire escape. I held the handrails tightly, and watched every step I took."

The dogs and I then went around the back of the building to a yard, big enough to accommodate a hockey rink and a baseball field. In one corner, there was a cone mounted on a tall pole. It looked like a large megaphone. "That's an air raid siren," I said. "Its purpose was to warn the residents of a possible nuclear attack. Once, a test of the siren was conducted during recess. The cone started to rotate, and blare an alarm so loud that my limbs went numb. The kids all ran to the back of the school and formed rows. When the alarm stopped, the school principal came outside and lectured us about the Soviet menace, and its arsenal of atomic bombs. She also urged us to be vigilant and prepare ourselves to repel any invasion. My friends and I formed militias, and rehearsed military drills in the park. We were well prepared. The enemy would have rued the day it tried to invade our community."

"There was an outdoor hockey rink in the middle of the yard. Weeknights, we played organized hockey. Although players wore some protective equipment like shin pads, padded gloves, shoulder pads, and a jockstrap, goalies didn't wear masks, and forwards didn't wear helmets. We protected ourselves by wearing toques."

"Weekends, we played shinny hockey without the pads. There were two rules: we couldn't raise the puck, and we couldn't give body checks."

"My parents drove me to the rink. I laced my skates inside a shed made of dry wood and heated by a wood stove. We fed the fire ourselves with logs in the shed. Once, we ran out of logs, and someone ripped a plank from the wall, broke it into pieces, and used the pieces to fuel the fire."

"After lacing my skates tightly, I went on the ice to join one of the teams. Everybody was allowed to play, regardless of age or ability. Even priests and brothers, the male equivalent of nuns, joined us on the ice. One day, a priest rammed his shoulder in my chest so hard that I lost my breath, and had to leave the ice to recuperate in the shed."

"We scored goals but did not count them. If one side was too strong, the two sides exchanged players. When my feet were cold, I left the ice and stood next to the wood stove in the shed."

"We played all day. At the end of the afternoon, my parents picked me up by car. When I took my seat at the back, I leaned forward and asked my mother if my cheeks were red. She looked back, smiled, and replied, 'As red as tomatoes.'"

# Chapter 21

Tommy was immersed in thought. "Claude," he said finally, "from an early age, you walked alone to school. You and your parents walked around town, but they only held your hand to avoid a hazard. You played hockey unsupervised. Yet, whenever you took us outside, you tied us to a leash. Why?"

"I'm surprised you ask," I said. "I thought you liked the leash. At home, when I reached for it, you stuck out your tongue and panted, waiting impatiently for me to put it on you. On walks, I used it to guide you, and you used it to guide me. Most of the time, the leash was loose between us."

"You're right. But I still want to know why you made us wear one."

"The reason was that I was afraid to lose you."

"Did you ever lose me?"

"No, but one night, I was convinced that you had run away. It was one of the coldest nights of the winter. You and I met Pierre and Richard at the ski hill. Richard and I spent the evening going up and down the runs, while you and Pierre watched us from the cafeteria at the bottom of the hill. At the end of the evening, I went to the car and put my equipment in the trunk. You were sitting on the front seat, and when I opened the car door, you jumped through my fingers and started to run around the parking lot. I lost sight of you and asked the people in the parking lot if they had seen you, but they all said no."

"Next to the parking lot, there were trees in deep, fluffy snow. I looked for your tracks in the snow and was relieved to see none. I asked people at the patrol hut, and the pro shop, but nobody had seen you. I went inside the ski lodge, announced to Pierre and Richard that you were lost, and asked them to help me find you. We all headed in different directions."

"A few minutes later, Richard waved at me, and said, 'Dad found Tommy.' I followed him to the cafeteria and met Pierre inside the vestibule. Smiling, he opened the door, and pointed at you inside the cafeteria, going from table to table, accepting food scraps from patrons, and licking their plates. I snuck up on you and tethered you. The patrons cheered and said goodbye to a friend they had just made."

Bobby said, "You checked everywhere except the cafeteria vestibule, which is the one place Tommy had spent all his time at the ski hill. It should have been the first place to check."

"Tommy," I continued, "there was another time I regretted my decision to untie your leash. You and I were hiking in a local park. It was a mix of forests, wetlands, and fields. When we started our walk, I untied your leash and watched you drift toward the shrubs, ferns, and trees. At first, you stayed close to me and sometimes looked around you to make sure that I was nearby. Then, without warning, you disappeared deep inside the forest. I tried to run after you, but the thick foliage blocked my view. I moved aimlessly among the trees, cursing myself for letting you loose."

"Finally, I heard a series of barks. They were faint but aggressive and persistent. I followed them, and a few minutes later, spotted you through the trees. You were next to a rustic wooden fence surrounding a ring with show-jumping obstacles. A horse was neighing, rearing, and shaking its front legs at you. A woman was mounted on the horse, holding its mane for dear life. I became worried for her safety. The horse was tall. If the woman lost her balance, she would fall a long way, and if the horse fell backward, it would roll over her."

"When she saw me, she yelled. Although I couldn't decipher the words, I felt unwanted. I steered you away from the ring. You kept barking, and shifting your head from side to side to get a better view of the horse."

"Once we were a safe distance, I looked back and saw that the horse was still agitated, but under control. The woman had dismounted and was standing next to it, holding the reins, and making it walk in a tight circle. Breathing a sigh of relief, I led you deeper into the forest."

"It was the first time that I had seen you taunt an animal for pleasure. This horse was at home, minding its own business, and you were trespassing on its property." I looked at Tommy, and raised my eyebrows, hoping to see an expression of remorse.

But Tommy turned to Bobby, and said, "I was just having fun."

"I wish I had been there," said Bobby. "How close were you to the horse? How often did it rear up? Would you be able to find the ring again? If we went there, could you bark at the horse from the front, while I nip its leg from behind?"

"We will not ever, ever go near that ring again," I vowed. "You asked why I kept you on a leash. Now, you know."

"I can understand why you kept Tommy on a leash. He was fit to be tied sometimes. But why did you keep me on a leash?"

"My dear Bobby," I replied, shaking my head, "you were even worse. One night, you made me run after you for more than an hour."

"Where?"

"At a park near our apartment. On one side of the park, there were tennis courts, and on the other side, there was a baseball field. Between them, there was a corridor leading to a busy street. The tennis courts were fully enclosed by a fence, but there was a gap in the fence of the baseball field to allow workers and their maintenance equipment to enter the field. Still, I took you to the baseball field because of its wider space."

"Until then, I had always kept you on a leash. But I decided to test your obedience."

"A blanket of wet snow covered the ground. After I untied the leash, you ran around me several times to celebrate your freedom. I called your name repeatedly, but you ignored me repeatedly."

"After a few minutes, you stopped and stared at me. I reached into my pocket, grabbed a treat, and threw it a few feet in front of me. When you took it, I jumped and tried to grab your collar, but you darted away. I spent the next few minutes luring you with treats, but you took them all without being captured."

"I had a tennis ball with me and threw it over your head. You ran after it, and retrieved it in the snow, then dropped it at my feet. I made no effort to grab your collar. Time after time, I threw the ball, and watched you retrieve it, then drop it near my feet, each time a little closer than the last. The more we played, the less guarded you became. Finally, you let me pat you on the shoulder. I decided to make my move."

"The next time you dropped the ball, I dove and managed to grab your collar. Kneeling in the snow, I hurried to tie the leash to the collar. 'Now I have you,' I thought. How wrong I was. You pulled back, and your head slipped through the collar. I was kneeling in the snow with the leash in one hand, and the collar in the other. You ran away again. Imagine how I felt."

"I was afraid you might notice the gap in the fence, and run toward the street, so I decided to lure you inside the tennis courts, where there was no gap. But to reach the tennis courts, you first had to cross the corridor, and there was no barrier between the corridor and the street. I noticed that the gate of the tennis courts was opened. I threw the tennis ball over the fence and watched you sprint through the gate to retrieve it. I then followed you inside the tennis courts and shut the gate."

"The ordeal ended as quickly as it had begun. You walked back to me with the ball in your mouth and lowered your head. I wrapped the collar around your neck and took a deep breath. You were mine again."

After a pause, I said, “Bobby, you escaped another time. Early one morning, I was driving you and Tommy to the daycare kennel, when I heard you whimper in the back seat. I decided to stop the car to see what was wrong. As soon as I opened the back door, you hopped out of the car and went trotting along the sidewalk, your leash dangling behind you. I ran after you, hoping to grab the leash.”

“When I got close, you veered toward the street. Alarmed, I ran toward the street, prepared to flag down cars.”

“But you backtracked, ambled down the sidewalk, and parked yourself next to a tree. I walked briskly toward you, but you veered toward the street again. When I jumped in front of the cars, the drivers greeted me rudely. They honked their horns or bypassed me. Some of them sped past me, probably suspecting that I wanted to hijack their car.”

“You returned to the sidewalk, and sat down, waiting for me. I grabbed the leash and led you to the car. You wagged your tail as if nothing had happened.”

“But something had happened. You had forced me to jump in front of moving cars. What do you have to say for yourself?”

“I was just having fun.”

# Chapter 22

"There must be at least one time you wished I had been off-leash," said Tommy.

"Nope. I can't think of one."

"What about the time you and I went rollerblading?"

"At the apartment?"

"No. You and I only went rollerblading once at the house before the apartment. I was still a puppy, full of youthful vigor, and although we walked every day, I also needed to run. One summer night, you decided to take me rollerblading. You laced up your skates, put the leash on me, and started to skate down the street. I ran by your side, and after a few strides, we were moving in sync. You were in a good mood. As we passed your neighbors on the street, you smiled and waved at them."

"Suddenly, I saw a cat, and gave chase, pulling you behind me. You managed to keep your balance but followed helplessly. I pulled harder and harder to keep up with the cat. Finally, it changed direction, jumped on someone's front lawn, and climbed up a tree. I also jumped on the lawn, but you tripped, fell, and rolled a few times. You never let go of the leash, so I was forced to stop also. You spent a few minutes looking for bruises, brushing yourself off, and convincing neighbors that you were fine. Then, you removed your skates, and walked home on your socks, grumbling all the way."

When Bobby stopped laughing, Tommy said, "If you think the last incident was funny, wait till you hear the next one."

Turning to me, he said, "It was the time you took me for a shoot at a professional studio inside a shopping mall. A salesman had sold you a coupon at our house that would entitle you to have the photographer take professional pictures at a discount. The studio was on the fourth floor of the mall."

"You were skeptical about dogs being permitted inside the mall, but the salesman informed you of an exception for patrons of the studio. They and their pets were entitled to use a service elevator in the basement garage that lifted them directly to the entrance of the studio. The salesman handed you a rough map of the basement and left the house."

"The day before the shoot, you hired a groomer to give me a shampoo and clip my nails. On the day itself, you brushed my coat until it was soft, bright, and shiny. Then, we left. You entered the basement garage of the mall and followed the directions on the map, which led to a janitor's closet, not a service elevator. Thinking that you might have read the map upside down, you drove to the other end of the garage, where you spotted the door of a service elevator, parked the car, and took me up the elevator."

"On the fourth floor, we saw shops of all kinds, including a clothing store, a shoe store, a health and beauty store, and a jewelry store. But there was no photography studio."

"You approached the person closest to you and asked her for directions to the studio. She pointed at the other end of the floor. You asked her if there was another studio at this end, closer to the service elevator, but she shook her head and explained that although there were two service elevators, there was only one studio, and the studio was at the other end of the floor, near the other service elevator."

"After thanking her, you checked your watch and noticed that there was no time left for you to ride down this elevator, traverse the basement garage, and ride up the other elevator. Besides, I was getting restless and fidgety. You decided to walk directly to the photography studio on the other side of the mall. You looked straight ahead and pretended I was your service dog. 'All I want you to do,' you whispered, 'is walk in a straight line until I find the studio.' But on my first trip ever to a shopping mall, I had other plans in mind."

"I stopped and lurched. I tried to run, but the floor was too slippery. I accosted shoppers and sniffed their bags. Some shoppers walked around us. Some turned and walked away. Some grumbled out loud. You kept apologizing, 'Please excuse my dog. He's still in training. This is not a good day for him.'"

"A kid threw me a treat which I snatched and swallowed without chewing. We zigzagged our way along the floor."

"Finally, you found the photography studio, but when you tried to steer me toward it, I tried to pull the other way. It was my first time window shopping, and I wanted to make the most of it. I wonder what the shoppers thought when they saw a master and his service dog pulling a leash in opposite directions as if they were having a tug of war."

"They must have thought, 'Some service dog,'" I said.

"Or else, some master," retorted Bobby.

"Finally, you used a treat to lure me toward the studio, where we met the photographer. While taking his pictures, he commented on how calm, and obedient I was. I saw your puzzled look. You wondered whether he was talking about me or another dog. Still, in the end, the pictures were beautiful. You bought several copies and sent them to friends and family as gifts."

"See what happens when you tie me to a leash?"

Bobby turned to me, and said, "I can think of another time that you were embarrassed. This time, there were three leashes, not just one. It was a very cold winter day. You took Tommy, Lexie, and me for a walk on a trail near Lexie's house. The sky was clear, and the sun was bright. The trail was icy, but the snow around the trees was fluffy. You stayed on the trail, while we wandered around you, our heads buried in the snow. As long as we were going in different directions, we tended to keep each other in check."

Then came a couple and their beautiful Golden Retriever. When they saw us, a man and three dogs, they took refuge behind a tree. We took no notice of them until the Golden Retriever barked.

Suddenly, we all looked up and charged at it. You had no chance. Our leashes pulled you off your feet. You landed on your stomach and slid helplessly along the icy path behind us.

"The snow flew in your face, and down your neck. You might have expected the dogs to fight, but as soon as we all met, we jumped and danced in the snow. Meantime, you got up and introduced yourself to the couple. 'We have to stop meeting like this', said the woman. 'Are you all right?' You replied that your pride hurt more than your limbs. You and the couple chatted about the cumulative strength of three dogs until I started barking. Smiling, you told them, 'Meeting adjourned.'"

Bobby concluded, "These embarrassing moments were brought to you courtesy of three dogs on leashes."

# Chapter 23

"I agree," I said. "I did suffer embarrassing moments when you were on a leash. But I also suffered embarrassing moments when you were off-leash, such as the time Tommy and I went to see another photographer."

Turning to Tommy, I said, "He had a studio in the attic of his home. When we entered his studio, he asked us to sit on a blanket in front of a screen. Then, he described the image he wanted to capture. We were to sit beside each other, look at him, and smile."

You and I complied immediately.

"'Perfect,' he said, 'hold it while I get ready.' He aimed his lamp at us, attached the camera to a stand, and adjusted the rings around the lens. But when he asked us to smile for the camera, you got up, sniffed my ears, licked my cheeks, and wagged your tail in my face. I pulled you toward me, pleading with you to behave. But you barked, rolled on your back, and kicked your feet in the air."

"The photographer waited patiently for you to quit clowning. After a few minutes, he groaned and suggested that we try a change of scenery. In his backyard, there was an old, majestic maple tree with a bough that extended horizontally. He asked me to sit on the bough and, if at all possible, have you sit at my feet. Again, you complied. 'Hold that pose,' he said, backing up toward his equipment. Instead, you followed him to his equipment. You sniffed the tripods, the rigs, and the stands. 'Can you call Tommy?' he asked."

"This is expensive equipment."

"I got up and coaxed you back with me on the bough."

"Exasperated, he started to snap pictures at random. He took one of your rump, one of your legs, and one of your tail. The camera kept clicking, and the pictures kept coming, but none of them were any good. Then, you assumed the perfect pose. This time, he pressed the shutter continuously, without looking through the lens. When the pictures appeared on his camera screen, he smiled. 'They're perfect,' he said. 'Come see for yourself. You'll be pleased.' And he was right."

"Your smile was especially attractive. Your lips curved up naturally, giving you a perpetual smile."

I paused, then said, "We can debate the utility of leashes all day, but I'm convinced that the leash once saved me from getting lost in the wilderness. Tommy, one fall weekend before Bobby was born, you and I went camping at a remote campground, deep in the forest. It was a cool, sunny afternoon. The days were getting shorter, and the evenings were getting colder. The leaves were changing color from green to bright yellow, red, and orange. In a few weeks, they would fall, and form a carpet of brown leaves."

Near the campground, there was a hiking trail, invisible from the ground, but marked by badges in the trees. We went hiking on the trail. As I gazed at the trees, the bushes, the leaves, and the fallen branches, you gazed at a deer standing on the other side of a clearing. You tried to sneak up on it, but the deer saw you from afar and hopped gracefully into the forest.

"I left the trail to meet you. We walked along the edge of the clearing, where we saw four more deer cross our path. They were close, and you tried to run after them, but they evaded you easily. You had to go around the bushes, and under the broken branches, whereas they just sprang over them. You abandoned the chase and came back."

"But where was the trail? Walking several feet in one direction, then several feet in another, I looked in vain for badges in the trees. The sun disappeared, and the badges became invisible anyway. The forest became a dark, cold, and spooky place. I was forced to concede to myself that we were lost. I started to visualize wild animals stalking us."

"After all," said Bobby, "you never know when you'll be attacked by wild chipmunks, wild turtles, and wild woodpeckers."

I pursed my lips and continued. "It was getting too dark to see, so I decided to put the leash on you. If we were lost, we'd be lost together. We walked and walked until suddenly, you crouched and refused to move. Thinking that you had detected the scent of a wild animal, I listened for unusual noises. But all was quiet. After a few seconds, I tried to resume the hike by gently pulling you, but you refused to budge until I pulled you in one particular direction. You jumped to your feet and took the lead. It occurred to me that you might know where you were going, so I decided to follow you. Whenever the leash became taut, I adjusted my direction."

“Finally, I heard the swish of tires on the pavement and realized that we were approaching a highway. We walked along the highway and found the campground in the middle of the night. You had followed your nose to safety.” Tommy nodded.

“Had you been off leash, you and I would have been separated, and I would never have found my way to the camp.”

“Thanks for the kind words,” said Tommy, “but we would never have been separated. Had I lost sight of you, I would have been able to find you by smelling you.”

I was stunned, and said, “I wish I had your keen sense of smell.”

“Until you grow a nose like ours,” quipped Bobby, “I suggest you buy yourself a compass and learn how to use it.”

# Chapter 24

I looked at my watch and saw that it was almost time to meet Andy at the boulder. We left the school grounds and walked briskly up the street. Suddenly, the weather worsened. The temperature dropped below freezing. It started to snow, and the landscape became a bland grey. Cars came to a stop on the side of the street. Pedestrians sought shelter. There were strong gusts of wind, and the wires on the telephone poles fluttered. We passed by the hospital, which was barely visible from our side of the street. “This is one nasty storm,” I told the dogs, “but it won’t last.”

The storm subsided by the time we reached the train station at the mouth of the park. A thick blanket of heavy snow covered the ground. Bobby and I walked effortlessly, but Tommy lagged. I sent Bobby ahead to meet Andy while I stayed with Tommy, who was trudging through the snow.

From a distance, we saw Andy standing several feet from the boulder. Wearing a coat, gloves, and boots, he was stalking a large, majestic elk near the trees. Weighing close to seven hundred lbs., the elk had large antlers. Its thick coat was a bright reddish brown. Its mane was black, and its rump was ivory.

When Tommy and I reached the boulder, we saw Bobby trying to pounce on the elk from different angles, but the elk was unaware of his presence. When he saw us approach, Bobby ran back to us.

"That was fun," he said.

By now, Tommy was limping noticeably.

Meantime, Andy was inching closer to the elk. Suddenly, he yelled at the top of his lungs and waved his arms wildly at the elk. Startled, it raised its head, pointed its antlers at Andy, and took a few steps in his direction. The tables had now turned. The elk was preparing to stalk Andy. Chills ran through me. Andy looked for an escape. The trees and houses were too far away. "Run for the boulder," I shouted. His eyes glued on the elk and he started to walk backward, but the elk followed him, step after step.

Andy turned swiftly and sprinted toward the boulder, the elk in hot pursuit. "Run, Andy, run," I yelled. He lumbered in the heavy snow but managed to reach the boulder first. He jumped on it and crawled to safety at the top. After circling the boulder, the elk stood on its hind legs, placed his front hoofs on the boulder, and stared at Andy, as if daring him to jump off the boulder. Its head was so close that Andy could feel its breath.

Suddenly, a snowball swished overhead and landed on the elk's shoulder. Its body shook, and it bolted away.

Andy looked over his shoulder and saw a boy walking toward him. "John!" he shouted, "Am I glad to see you! You're my best brother after Luc and Pierre. I was scared, really scared. It's a good thing you came." When John reached the boulder, they embraced.

"I wonder if John aimed his snowball at Andy," said Bobby, "and hit the elk by accident."

"Let's go to the fort," Andy told John.

"We can't stay for long. Dad sent me to get you. He wants to leave soon."

"We still have time to throw a few snowballs at cars."

As John walked up a hill, Andy turned to us, and whispered, "You better stay here. John can't see or hear you, and if I start talking to you, he'll think I'm talking to myself."

Andy grinned and said, "You can watch us throw snowballs at cars from here." Andy and John ran to the top of the hill and hid behind the snowfort. It was just a wall of packed snow, a few feet high.

"They'll only be targeting cars that are speeding," I told the dogs. "I remember the thrill of watching my snowball spin through the air, locked on its target. After their cars were struck, the drivers often stopped to look for dents. They then turned around to hurl insults at us. But we weren't afraid of them. We knew we could outrun them."

Suddenly, Andy popped up and hurled a snowball at us. I had no time to react and the snowball flew right through my chest. "Why did you do that?" asked John. "You just wasted a perfectly good snowball."

"Don't worry. I'll make another one."

"Hey, look! There's a car coming our way. Quick, hide before the driver sees us. Get ready!"

The two boys crouched behind the wall. When the car moved past them, they stood up, took aim, and hurled the snowballs. Both struck the side of the car. The driver stopped, rolled down his window, shook his fist at the boys, then drove away.

A few minutes later, a second car sped past them, and the boys threw two more snowballs. One sailed over the car, but the other one struck the side mirror, shattering it into pieces that made clinking noises when they hit the pavement. The car kept moving.

The boys cheered.

"I hit the car," bragged Andy.

"No, I hit the car," countered John.

They argued back and forth.

"What was so thrilling about throwing snowballs at moving cars?" asked Tommy.

I shrugged my shoulders.

There was a pause. "Come to think of it," I said, "We also threw rocks at freight trains. I had a cousin who lived near railroad tracks. On the other side of the tracks, there was a rock formation. He and I went to the formation to throw rocks at trees, and telephone poles. When we heard train whistles, we waited for the trains to pass us. If they were freight trains, we threw rocks at the wagons. They were made of heavy steel, and our rocks just bounced off them. We never threw rocks at passenger trains."

Suddenly, we saw two men creep up on Andy and John. The men tackled them before they could react. Andy was subdued with little effort, but John defended himself vigorously. He pulled, squirmed, twisted, and even threw punches. But the man was heavier, and soon gained the upper hand. He restrained John with a firm headlock.

The man asked, "Which one of you broke my mirror?"

His voice muffled, John asked, "I beg your pardon?"

"You heard me. Who threw the snowball?"

"I can't hear you with your arm over my ears."

"Both of them were bragging about hitting the mirror," said his friend. "We should teach both of them a lesson."

"John said, 'I'm the one who threw the snowball. Let me go."

"Let you go?"

"No, let me go."

"That's what I said."

"I thought you said, 'Let me go.'"

"Don't answer," said his friend. "He's toying with you." Incensed, the man flipped John on his back and held him down.

A woman who lived in a house adjacent to the snowfort stepped on her balcony. "That's enough," she yelled. "I just called the police, and an officer will be here any minute."

One of the men protested, "But they just broke my car mirror." "I don't care. Tell the police."

Frustrated, the men looked at each other, gave the boys one last shove, and decided to leave.

Andy and John tried to thank the woman for her timely intervention, but she waved her hand, and said, "Never mind. Last winter, I watched you throw snowballs at cars. But not this year. The next time I see you here, I'll call the police myself. I'm serious." Embarrassed, Andy and John bowed their heads and left.

At the bottom of the hill, John urged Andy to follow him home. "Go ahead. I'll be right behind you."

John left, and Andy joined the dogs and me. Shaken, he said, "I'll never throw another snowball at a car."

Then, he grinned, and added, “But I might throw rocks at freight trains. When you hit the wagons, the trains keep moving, and their conductors don’t jump out of locomotives to chase you.”

# Chapter 25

Andy frowned. "What is the matter?" asked Tommy.

"I'm confused," he replied. "I seem to be remembering events from the future, instead of events from the past. Why do I remember smashing the pane of glass at school; memorizing a cheat sheet in the library; studying for the wrong exam; and altering my grades? None of these events have occurred to me yet."

"Good question," said Tommy, pausing then adding, "After all, when you describe a past event, you remember it. When you describe a future event, you predict it."

"Also, when you remember an event, you know you're not predicting it, and when you predict an event, you know you're not remembering it. Remembering and predicting are two distinct feelings."

"Of course," said Bobby, as he turned to Andy, and said, "You're confused because when you describe a future event, you know you should be predicting it, but instead, you know you're remembering it."

Andy nodded.

"Describe another future event," said Tommy, "and include as many details as possible. Tell us what you feel."

Andy nodded, and said, “Two years from now, when Claude is twelve years old, his parents will visit friends for a weekend, and take him, John, and Pierre with them.”

“The friends will have two sons of their own. During the day, the five boys will play in the woods next to the house, and at night, they’ll go camping on the edge of the woods. They’ll assemble the tent themselves. They’ll clear the debris; unfold the canvas; nail the stakes in the ground; install a center pole; lift the canvas; unfold their sleeping bags inside the tent. They’ll explore the forest until dark, then return to their tent and talk.”

“Late that at night, Claude will hear a ruffling noise outside the tent, raise his hand to get everyone’s attention, and ask, ‘Did you hear that noise?’ The boys will look at each other, and nod nervously.”

“Everyone will agree that someone should look outside, but everyone will refuse to look, and everyone will explain why someone else should look. ‘You heard the noise, you look.’ ‘But you’re the strongest, you look.’ ‘But you’re the oldest you look.’”

Suddenly, one of the sides of the tent will collapse.

“Four-year-old Pierre will get up, and step outside. He’ll let out a piercing shriek, dart through the door, and yell at the top of his lungs, ‘Two men! Two men!’ He’ll fling himself into Claude’s arms for protection.”

“Will Claude ask Pierre to go outside to have a second look?” asked Bobby.

Andy shook his head. “No, he won’t have time. The men will appear at the doorway. They’ll laugh, and say, ‘Relax, boys, relax. It’s just us, your dads. We were kidding.’”

"Claude will say, 'Dad! I am relaxed. I was only kidding too. I knew it was you all along.'"

"The men will return to the house. The boys will stay inside the tent, but spend the rest of the night wide awake, listening for noises. They'll also take turns roll-calling each other to make sure that all of them are still awake. They'll fall asleep at daybreak." I listened in awe as Andy recounted the event.

Tommy asked, "When you were describing this future event, did you feel you were remembering it, or predicting it?"

"I was definitely remembering it."

"I can't believe you kicked your little brother out of the tent," chided Bobby.

"Pierre went outside on his own before I was able to stop him."

"Except," said Andy, "Claude will throw his little brother out of the house two years later. When Claude is fourteen years old, his family will move to a house very close to a high school. One afternoon, he'll see a few students loitering in the backyard, and send Pierre to confront them."

"Claude will push him out the back door, and egg him on. Fists clenched, Pierre will run toward them, yelling, 'Get off my property, you kids.' At the time, the students will be twice Pierre's age, twice his height, and twice his weight, but impressed with his gall, they'll apologize to him, and leave promptly."

"Can you remember other events showcasing Claude's passivity in the face of adversity?" asked Bobby.

"Oh yes," said Andy, "I have a library brimming with events. About a year later, Claude's parents will visit relatives in a city, and stay at a luxurious hotel. Claude and John will go for a swim in the pool at the hotel. Three bullies will jump in the water, call Claude names, and splash water in his face. Claude will just back away. Meantime, John will walk up to one of them, and slap him across the face, not once but twice. Stunned, the bully will turn around, and jump out of the pool, followed closely by his friends."

Andy looked at me. "I'm not sure I like my older self," he said.

"I wish I could grow up to be Pierre or John."

"Don't worry. In time, you'll blossom into Claude the man."

"Like the time you were brave when the priest at your school slapped you across the face?" asked Andy.

"But the priest was a person of authority," I replied.

"This I have to hear," said Bobby. "Why would a priest have to slap Claude across the face?"

"Claude will attend a boarding school run by the priests," said Andy. "At the school, there will be an auditorium in the basement of a building, large enough to hold all the students. The teachers and priests will be seated on an elevated stage. The students will be seated in chairs on the floor. There will only be one exit door."

"Late one afternoon, the priests will call a meeting, probably to make an example of a student who has broken a rule. One of them will address the students. When he's done, he'll look around the room, and say, 'Before you go, I have something important to say, and I want you to listen very carefully. The exit door behind you is very narrow.

You cannot all possibly fit through it at the same time. If you try, you'll crush one another. WALK! DON'T RUN!' He'll pause for effect, then dismiss the students."

"All the students will jump out of their seats, and race for the exit door. It will be dinnertime. They'll be hungry, and anxious to be among the first to form the queue in the cafeteria."

"But the students will have a surprise waiting for them. As they converge on the exit door, another priest hiding behind it will jump in front of them, and slam the door behind him. The students will pile into each other."

"What did he just tell you? WALK! DON'T RUN!"

"Claude will turn to the student beside him and shout, 'WALK! DON'T RUN!' Incensed, the priest will raise his hand, and with a wide swing, smack Claude across the face, nearly knocking him down. His cheeks will throb, and his ears will sting. He'll rub them to ease the pain. He'll look at the priest, but the priest will stare him down, then ask the others, 'Does anyone else have anything to add to the discussion?' The students will bow their heads submissively."

'When I open these doors,' he'll add, 'I want to see you, each and every one of you, walk out the door, one by one. Do you hear me?' The students will nod. He'll ask again. 'Yes,' they'll shout in unison.

"Finally, he'll open the door, but the students will stay put until he motions for them to move. As instructed, they'll shuffle through the door slowly. Outside, they'll start to run for the cafeteria, except Claude, who will continue to walk, in case other priests are watching him."

The students will tease Claude, as they run past him. He'll be the last student to arrive at the cafeteria. Sulking, he'll stand at the back of the queue, plotting his revenge.

"Later that night, Claude will call his father, the school inspector, to complain, and ask him to punish the priest, maybe even fire him, but his father will interrupt him. 'I know what happened,' he'll say. 'The priest called me this afternoon, and told me that he had to punish you because you had been disrespectful.' Claude will try to give his side of the story, but his father will refuse to listen."

"The incident bothered me for years," I said, interrupting Andy. "Decades later, I asked my mother if she remembered it. She nodded, and said, 'What you should know is that your father warned the priest never, ever to touch you, or any other student, again. But he couldn't tell you because the priest had made a good point. You had undermined his authority and deserved a reprimand. You received your reprimand. He received his warning.'"

# Chapter 26

"Will I be a coward all my life?" asked Andy. "Whenever someone bullies me, will I never be brave enough to defend myself?"

I put my hand on his shoulder, and replied, "When you blossom into Claude the man, you'll be brave enough."

"Will I blossom into Claude the man before I'm thirty-five years old?"

"Yes, of course."

"Then, why will I let Romeo bully me?"

I blushed. The Romeo incident had occurred when I was thirty-five years old. I could no longer pretend to be a boy.

"Who is Romeo?" asked Bobby.

"Romeo will be a man looking for Juliet," replied Andy. "One summer night, when Claude is living in an apartment on the second floor of a house, he'll be awakened by a tapping noise. Someone on the ground will be throwing pebbles at his bedroom window to get his attention. Claude will crawl out of bed, pull the curtains, and see a man standing in the alleyway below, and hear him say, 'Hey Juliet. It's me, Romeo. I'm back. Open the door. I want to see you. I want to express my love to you.'"

“Claude will take a step back, wondering how to respond.”

“I know you’re in there. I just saw the curtains move. Open the door. I have a gift for you.”

“You have a gift?”

“Yes, the gift of love.”

“Not tonight. I have a headache.”

“My gift will fix your headache.”

After a brief pause, Romeo’s tone will change. “Hey, what’s wrong with your voice?”

“I have a cold.”

“Romeo will yell, ‘Who are you? You’re not Juliet. What are you doing in Juliet’s bedroom?’”

“Claude will stick his head outside, and say, ‘It’s not what you think.’”

“When he sees Claude, Romeo will freeze for a moment, then run to the back of the house, scoot up the stairs, and pound on the door. When there’s no answer, he’ll pound harder. Finally, Claude will open the door before the noise awakens his neighbor. Romeo’s eyes will narrow. He’ll storm past Claude, and inspect the rooms in the apartment while calling Juliet’s name. He’ll even look in the closets. When he’s inside the bedroom, he’ll notice the curtains waving in the wind, and say, ‘She must have jumped out of the window.’ He’ll take a swing at Claude, who will duck. Romeo will stumble.”

“I hope you threw Romeo out of the window,” Bobby said.

“Are you kidding?” asked Andy. “After he misses, Romeo will take another swing, but Claude’s neighbor will appear out of nowhere, block the blow, and tackle Romeo.

Both men will fall heavily on the floor. After a brief skirmish, the neighbor will pin Romeo to the floor."

"Let me go. I just caught him sleeping with Juliet."

"'Juliet is gone. She left soon after you left. She was so distraught that she went looking for you. You should go find her.' There was a pause in the action."

"Where do you think she went?"

"Start with the place you went after you left her."

"Romeo will nod, pick himself up, and leave, determined to find his Juliet before she dies of loneliness."

Andy looked a little glum.

Tommy asked him, "Why the long face?"

"I feel guilty about telling you and Bobby about these events. I'm humiliating Claude. I should be minding my own business."

"Don't worry," said Tommy. "We're all family. Nobody else will know. Bobby and I will never tell any other dog."

"There's another problem. I've had a few glimpses of my future, and I don't like what I see. I don't like the person I'll become."

"If I were you," replied Tommy, "I would be gentler on Claude. He might not be an action hero, but is he the coward that you pretend to be? I think he's a person who is cautious. When the priest slapped him in the face, he told his father. What else could he do? Curse the priest, and slap him in the face too? In those days, persons of authority were allowed to administer corporal punishment, if it was proportionate. Slapping a disrespectful student was still considered a proportionate response. 'Spare the rod, spoil the child.' Corporal punishment is not tolerated today, but you can't judge the actions of the past by the norms of today. Claude spoke to his father, and his father reprimanded the priest. It was all that Claude could expect."

"And Pierre stepped outside the tent before Claude could stop him. He didn't push him outside, or ask him to look. Should Claude have gone outside himself? Maybe, if Pierre had remained outside, but he jumped right back into the tent. Claude was still assessing the danger. 'Discretion is the better part of valor.' Was the trespasser a squirrel, a cat, or a dog? Or was it a bear, a bobcat, or a wolf?"

"But when the tent collapsed," said Andy, "Claude had to know that the trespassers were people and not wild animals."

Tommy agreed, but noted, "How many people were there? What was their purpose? What would be their next move? Were the boys still safer in the tent?"

"So what if Claude stepped back when the bully in the pool splashed water in his face? So what if he ducked when Romeo threw a punch at him? Neither one had injured him. There was still hope that he could defuse the confrontations without retaliating. 'Violence begets violence.'"

"I applaud John and the neighbor for coming to Claude's aid. Both acted bravely. But their actions were not the only options available to Claude. I for one, refuse to be too critical of him. I think his actions reflect caution, not cowardice."

Tommy turned to Andy, and said, "When animals are threatened, they have two options: fight or flight. We either fight the threat, or we take flight. But people have other options, and one of them involves the use of speech. Sometimes, they can diffuse a conflict just by talking."

“Let me give you an example. One day, Claude and I were walking along a street in a neighborhood. I felt the urge to do my business and went to someone’s front lawn to squat. Claude pulled a plastic bag from his pocket and waited for me to finish. Suddenly, a man appeared from nowhere, and ran toward me, yelling, ‘Stop! Stop! Stop!’ But I was past the point of no return. I had to stay, stay, stay till I was done. I felt helpless, unable to defend myself. All I could do was watch him charge at me. The man was livid. I’m sure he was determined to kick me or drag me in the street. The closer he came, the louder he yelled. He was within a few feet of me when Claude stepped between us and stuck out his hand. The man stopped. He and Claude stared at each other icily.”

“Claude said, ‘I have a plastic bag with me, and I’ll pick up the stools when my dog is finished. You’ll just have to wait. I’m not dragging him anywhere.’”

“But the man was belligerent. Taking another step toward him, he said, ‘If you won’t stop your dog, then I will. Give me the leash.’”

Claude shook his head and took one step toward him. They stood face-to-face.

“Then, to my pleasant surprise, Claude started to give the man a lecture about boundaries.”

“‘This spot,’ he said, pointing at the patch on which I was squatting, ‘is not even part of your lawn. It’s part of the street.’”

“No. The street ends at the curb. The rest of the property is mine.”

"No, sir. The pavement ends at the curb. The street ends somewhere behind you. Check your building location survey. You'll see."

"My what?"

"'Your building location survey. It's a professional drawing of the boundaries of your property. A surveyor prepared the drawing when your house was built. Your lawyer sent you a copy of the survey with the reporting letter when you bought the house. Have a look at it.' The man was at a loss for words."

"His wife came to the door holding a large envelope, and said, 'I have the lawyer's package with me.'"

"He turned around and went to meet his wife and inspect the package. There was a delay, a short one, but long enough for Claude to pick up my stools, and escape. The point is he managed to diffuse the conflict by distracting the man for a few seconds."

Andy smiled. "As we speak, I can recall another instance in which Claude will resolve a public hazard with words. At the time, he'll be a doorman at a hotel. He'll greet guests in the driveway, and carry their luggage into the lobby. Late one night, while he's on duty, he'll notice a pick-up truck moving erratically on the street. Somehow, the driver will manage to steer his truck in the hotel driveway, come to a stop, and roll down the window. His breath will reek of alcohol, his eyes will be bloodshot, and his skin will be flushed."

"He'll mumble something unintelligible. When Claude asks him to repeat himself, he'll show Claude an empty beer bottle, and mumble, 'Beer, beer.' Claude will try to dissuade him by offering to park his truck and walking him to the hotel bar. But the driver will shake his head, and repeat the words, 'Beer, beer.'"

"When he sees that the driver is adamant, Claude will point to the police station, located next to the hotel, and say, 'The beer store is in that building.' Suspicious, the driver will ask, 'Cop shop? Cop shop?'"

"Claude will reply, 'The police station is on the first floor. The beer store is in the basement. Ring the doorbell at the back door. Someone will greet you, and happily show you the beer store in the basement.' The driver will grunt, roll up his window, and drive his truck to the police station. After parking the truck, he'll stumble to the back door. An officer will greet him, and happily show him the jail cell in the basement."

Andy and the dogs chuckled.

"When Claude starts his shift on the next afternoon, the bell captain will summon him, and say, 'This morning, a guest of the hotel claimed that you sent him to jail last night. He said that he had a score to settle with you.'"

"I didn't know he was a hotel guest, but had I known, I would have given him the same directions."

The bell captain will suggest, "You better take the day off work. He'll check out of the hotel tomorrow morning, and drive home at the other end of the country. He won't be back anytime soon."

"And as Claude leaves the hotel, the bell captain will laugh and wink. Bobby smiled, and said, I can think of a story myself."

"'I'm not sure I want to hear it,' I protested."

"Don't worry. I know I've been teasing you all day, but this time, I'll be kind to you." Turning to Andy, he said,

"Claude and I were walking on a narrow footpath used by people and dogs alike. A teenaged girl in cutoff jeans was rollerblading behind us. As she overtook us, I turned around, and accidentally nudged her leg with my nose, leaving a wet mark. The girl didn't wince. She just went to sit on a bench, and scratched her leg with her fingernails, leaving pink marks on her skin."

"Moments later, a woman accosted us from behind. Visibly upset, she said, 'Your dog bit my daughter.'"

"No. My dog nudged your daughter with his nose."

"The woman became angry. She pointed to the scratch marks, and said, 'His nose did not leave these marks on her leg.'"

"Neither did his teeth. Your daughter's fingernails left these marks on her leg."

"Furious, the woman asked, 'Are you calling me a liar?' Claude remained silent. Raising her voice, she asked again, 'Are you calling me a liar?' Walkers in the park overheard her and looked our way. Two of them stopped to ask her if there was a problem. I became agitated and started to bark. The confrontation was escalating."

"To my surprise, Claude faced the woman, and said, 'I understand your concern for your daughter. I even share it. But the fault is mine, not the dog's. Although he did not bite her, his nose did nudge her, and even a nudge was unacceptable. I should never have allowed my dog to get so close to her. From now on, I'll make sure to keep him a safe distance from people by walking him exclusively on the grass.' Turning to the girl, he added, 'I'm sorry.'"

"The woman hesitated and looked at her daughter's leg one more time. Then, she put her arm around her daughter, and both left. She had made her point. Claude accepted it. The small gathering dispersed. Claude and I finished our walk on the grass."

Tommy took Andy aside, and said, "How do you feel now?"

"I feel better. Claude tricked the drunk driver and the irate homeowner. And he was remorseful toward the mother and her daughter. But someday, I hope to do more. Someday, I hope to do something great."

Tommy put an arm around Andy, and said, "Soon, you will do something great, I know it."

His face beaming with joy, Andy asked, "Really? When?"

"Soon."

# Chapter 27

After a short pause, Bobby turned to Tommy, and said, “Before I forget, I want you to comment on a rumor I heard about you. Apparently, you once chased a rabbit in the neighborhood, cornered it after much effort, but let it go. Tell me it isn’t so.”

Tommy nodded, and said, “But it is so. The rumor is true. One night, Claude and I were walking together when I spotted a rabbit on one of the front lawns. When it saw me, the rabbit fled to the back of the property, ran through backyards, and crawled under fences. But eventually, I caught up to it and cornered it against a wall. It froze, resigned to its fate.”

“You can run from Tommy,” said Bobby, “but you cannot hide. What did you do next?”

“I tagged it with my nose, then ran away, hoping it would tag me back. But when I turned around to look, I saw that it was gone. I looked for it briefly, then rejoined Claude.” Bobby looked puzzled.

I turned to Tommy, and said, “You were kind to smaller animals, even ones that tormented you. Do you remember the cat that lived on our street? We passed by its house on our way home. When it saw you coming down the street, it parked itself on the curb and taunted you by ignoring you."

When you first noticed it, you lifted your head, and the hairs on your back rose. You glared at it and panted. When you were close, you barked and lunged. Sometimes, you pulled so hard that the leash almost choked you. But that despicable cat was unflappable. If you only knew how much I resented it. Yelling and stomping my feet, I tried to scare it away, but it feared me even less.

"One day, as you and I were approaching the cat, I wondered if once, just once, I should let you chase it. I looked up and down the street for traffic, and saw that the coast was clear. So, I dropped the leash. You exploded across the street in two bounds, and pounced on the cat before it could react."

Bobby's eyes widened, and he asked Tommy, "Did you bite it?"

"No, I just tagged it."

Bobby looked bewildered.

"Tommy," I continued, "you were even kind to animals that hurt you. Julie was a good friend of mine. She and I worked on the same floor of a business. Her office was at one end of the floor, and my office was at the other end. Between the two offices, there was a boardroom. Julie had a puppy named Lexie. One day, Julie and I brought you and Lexie to work and put both of you in the boardroom."

"You were friends, and sometimes met at the park, but Lexie was a puppy with limitless energy, whereas you were a full-grown dog with limited patience. At the park, you could easily slip away, but in the boardroom, you had nowhere to hide. Nevertheless, I was convinced that you would never hurt her. After all, you were always kind to smaller animals that posed no threat to you."

"For a few minutes, all seemed peaceful in the boardroom. I could hear the snarling noises that dogs make when they play. But soon, I heard piercing shrieks. *Oh dear,* I thought, *Tommy is attacking the puppy.* Julie and I rushed to the boardroom but were shocked to see that you were the dog in agony. Lexie had sunk her puppy teeth in your ear and was hanging from your ear like an earring. Fortunately, Julie was able to remove the earring by coaxing it with treats."

Tommy and Bobby both winced.

"You never fought defenseless animals," I continued, "but you certainly fought dogs that attacked you."

"There was a big, black Newfoundlander dog that lived on our street. It was twice your size, and mean too. You were still a puppy then. If it saw you from its living room window, it barked ferociously while you were in view. If it saw you on the street, it barked and tried to charge at you."

"When I saw the dog, I turned back or went to the other side of the street. There was no animosity between its owner and me. When we crossed paths, we smiled at each other politely."

"One night, you and I left the house to begin our walk, when we heard the dog bark. It was coming in our direction. Its owner was an elderly man in his seventies who could barely control it at the best of times. *Here we go again*, I thought. The man rolled the leash around his hand to secure his grip, but the dog kept pulling him forward. I tried to coax you back inside the house, but you were in no mood to back down. Facing him, you stood tall and rigid and held your tail up high. The hairs on your back rose. You growled, exposed your teeth, and assumed a pose of readiness."

"The old man stumbled, dropped the leash, and fell heavily on the ground. The dog charged, but when it was close, you lunged at it. It veered away to avoid contact. Like a bull in an arena, it stopped, turned around, and charged again. Undaunted, you lunged at it again, but your leash stopped you. At that moment, I dropped the leash, and when the dog charged a third time, you pounced on it and bit its leg. It yelped in pain and limped toward its owner who grabbed the leash and walked his dog home."

This fight was over in an instant and taught me two lessons.

The other dog's bark was worse than its bite.

Your bite was worse than your bark.

I smiled at Tommy, and said, "Not only did you protect yourself from dogs, you also protected me from dogs."

"I always considered the next incident a little peculiar. It was the first and only time that a dog ever attacked me when I was walking a dog."

"You and I were enjoying a leisurely stroll in a neighborhood when a car turned into the driveway of one of the houses. The driver opened the back door, and a large poodle jumped out of the car."

"As soon as it noticed us, it charged. I was on the other side of the street, and you were on the other side of me. I expected the poodle to run around me to get to you, but to my surprise, it sprang straight for me. As I raised my arm in self-defense, I noticed your shadow from the corner of my eye ramming that poodle right in the gut, sending it reeling onto its back. You yourself spun in the air and landed heavily on the pavement. The poodle got up and staggered home. You got up and looked around for it. By then, it was hiding behind its owner, and taking refuge in its house. I bent on one knee and lavished you with gratitude."

"The poodle attacked me, not you. It wanted to bite me, not you. It might have done its damage, and gone straight home without looking at you. But you intervened and risked serious injury to yourself to protect me from serious injury."

"Saving me from a large dog is one thing," I continued, "but saving me from a skunk is quite another. One hot, summer night, I was sitting in a chair on the balcony of my house, reading a book while you slept at my feet."

"A skunk wobbled to the foot of the stairs. I never noticed it, but you were jarred from your sleep. As you crouched to jump on it, I grabbed your leash and held you back. The skunk sprayed the railing of the balcony, but some drops deflected on you. It took me several shampoos to remove the stench."

It was Bobby's turn. "Tommy," he said, "I was less than one year old when Claude hired a friend to hang some paintings in his living room. His friend brought his dog with him so it could play in the backyard with us while he worked. I'll call the dog a mutt, for so it was. When the friend arrived, Claude introduced the mutt to us. You were too busy chewing a bone to take notice. The mutt and I started roughhousing."

"Claude supervised us from the porch. Three dogs in a confined space is a recipe for hostility."

"The bone caught my attention, and I withdrew. I snuck up on you from behind and stole the bone from you. It was too heavy for me to lift, so I dragged it along the ground to another corner of the yard. As I was licking the bone, the mutt snuck up on me from behind, snatched it, and did a victory lap around the yard, displaying the bone in its jaws."

I said, "Imagine a dog sneaking up on another dog from behind and stealing its bone. How despicable."

Ignoring my comment, Bobby added, "Tommy, when you heard me whimpering, you ran across the yard and challenged the mutt. It promptly dropped the bone. You both growled, snarled, and barked with a fierceness that I had never witnessed before. Then, you lunged at each other. The skirmish was as brief as it was intense. Claude intervened immediately, but even then, your ear was bleeding. Yet, you were still eager to fight and kept lunging at the mutt. The mutt was eager to withdraw. Claude struggled to keep the two of you apart, until his friend rushed outside, and restrained his mutt while Claude restrained you."

"That day," said Bobby, "I learned that I had to stay in the fight until the other dog withdrew, even if it drew first blood."

# Chapter 28

There was a pause, then Bobby said, “Enough about Tommy. Let’s talk about me.”

I said, “Good idea. Bobby, I always thought that you were as brave as Tommy and as fierce as Tommy. But you were less discriminating than Tommy.”

“What do you mean?”

“For one thing, when you were a pup, you sometimes bit more than you could chew. Once, you engaged a dog that was too big and strong for you, and it pinned you to the ground. No dog ever pinned me to the ground. But it did, not once, but twice.”

“It happened one winter morning at the first daycare kennel that you and Tommy ever attended. The owner had given me the security code for the kennel because I dropped you off before business hours. After unlocking the front door, I went inside with you but left the door ajar so Tommy could linger outside for a few minutes.”

“The front door opened to a vestibule, and inside the vestibule, another door opened to a dormitory.”

“When you and I entered the dormitory, we were met by King, a large King Shepherd dog that had jumped outside its pen during the night. Strong and mature, it had a broad chest and a thick tail. It was tall and heavy, but fit."

"You circled King cheekily, stood behind it for a few seconds, then nipped its hind leg. King turned and jumped on your back. You collapsed, your legs outstretched in different directions."

"I pulled King off you."

"What did you expect?" asked Bobby. "The floor was slippery."

"Undaunted, you got up, shook yourself off, circled King, and lingered behind it. King remained still but gave you the side-eye. Then, you nipped its other hind leg. King turned around and pinned you against the floor, but this time, it also squeezed its mouth around the back of your neck."

"I yanked King off you."

"Although King was a docile dog, I wanted to avoid another confrontation, so I put you inside your cage in the dormitory. When I returned to the vestibule, I felt a rush of cold air and saw that the front door was wide open. Tommy had pushed it open with his forehead. He was waiting for me inside the vestibule, but King was gone."

"My heart sank. I ran outside and looked up and down the kennel, but saw no sign of King. I also looked up and down the street, but saw no sign of King. Then, spotting tracks in the snow, I followed them to a tree, where it had just finished relieving itself. I approached it quietly, grabbed its mane, and led it inside the kennel. It offered no resistance."

"In passing, I must say that King was an impressive creature. You had nipped its legs twice, and I had grabbed its mane thrice. Not once did King retaliate."

"Moreover, you were so keen to fight that you fought strangers and friends alike."

"You mean trespassers," countered Bobby.

"One evening in winter, you and I were walking on the sidewalk when a boy approached us from behind and passed us. You jumped and bit him on the arm. Luckily, he was wearing a thick coat, and your teeth didn't break his skin."

"Which is why I bit him," said Bobby.

"Then, on another winter evening, you and I were standing on a sidewalk while I was talking to a friend. A man approached us and extended his hand to you in friendship. But you nipped it. Luckily, he was wearing gloves, and your teeth didn't draw blood."

"Which is why I nipped him."

"And at daybreak one summer morning, you and I went for a walk. The air was crisp, and the birds were chirping. Near our home, there was a footpath that was flanked by countless shrubs. I usually avoided it because it was popular with pedestrians, cyclists, and skateboarders. But it was early, and I took a chance."

"As we strolled along the footpath, you sniffed every shrub we passed. I watched you closely to make sure that you were sniffing, and not foraging."

"Then, two joggers turned a corner. As I looked up, I heard the ruffling of twigs. Before I could take a firm hold of the leash, you jumped on one of the joggers, bit into his tank top shirt, and ripped a long strip off it. The jogger stopped, and lifted his shirt, exposing his side. There was a small scratch on his skin, but no blood."

"'Your dog just bit me!' he yelled. 'Your dog just bit me!'"

*I heard you the first time!* I thought. *I heard you the first time!*

"Now, I have to go to the hospital."

"He gave his name. Imagining a dog catcher coming to my home to take you away, I gave him a false name and a false address. When I got home, I contacted the local health department and gave it my correct name and my correct address. I also delivered a copy of your record of vaccinations to prove that you were compliant with all the regulations. There were no repercussions."

"And last but not least, you scared your friends."

"You and I were waiting for the elevator in the basement vestibule. When the elevator door opened, a man and his daughter, a two-year-old toddler, stepped out. When he heard you bark, he pulled his daughter back into the elevator. I held you against the wall, but you slipped out of your collar, and scampered inside the elevator, as the door was shutting. By the time I reached the elevator, the door was closed. I pressed the button, and slowly, too slowly, the door reopened."

"I looked inside the elevator and saw the man standing in the corner, shielding his daughter from you. Your paws resting on the railing, you stood beside them. I wrapped the collar around your neck, apologized, and pulled you out of the elevator. We left the basement by the garage door."

"Claude, you're being unfair," Andy countered. "Bobby will not scare the little girl. That night, you'll pay the man a visit at his apartment. The man will confirm that neither he nor his daughter was injured. 'At first,' he'll say, 'I was concerned, and took my daughter back inside the elevator. But then, I realized he was friendly. He never snarled or growled. He just stood next to us and stuck out his tongue. My daughter was amused. Since then, she has been sticking out her tongue at us. She has also been asking us for a puppy. We might buy her one after we teach her to stop sticking out her tongue at us. All because of Bobby.'"

"I agree," said Tommy. "Bobby was just overly exuberant."

"He might have ripped the jogger's shirt, but he didn't bite the jogger. And how was he supposed to know whether the jogger was a friend or foe? He did what any good dog would do: defend the pack, and ask questions later. You should be grateful."

"Besides, I once made the same mistake myself."

Turning to Bobby, he said, "At the time, Claude had a law office on the ground floor of a building. The office was a large room, about the size of a tennis court, and divided in the middle by a long corridor. On one side of the corridor, there was a column of offices for the lawyers, and on the other side, there was a column of workstations for their assistants. Each workstation had a desk and a metal cabinet."

"Usually, Claude worked from his office. However, on this day, he worked from the workstation because his assistant was absent."

"When I was a puppy, we spent the whole day in the office. We started the workday by playing fetch. Claude threw a toy down the corridor, and I retrieved it. One day, the toy bounced under a desk. I emerged from the desk with a shoe belonging to one of the assistants. I thought it was a toy. When I dropped it at Claude's feet, he saw that the shoe was speckled with teeth marks. He had to buy the assistant a new pair of shoes."

"I slept on a cushion in the workstation, my leash tied to the filing cabinet. One day, three men entered the office and confronted him. I had never seen any of them before. He and the men stood face-to-face and stared at each other. Then, one of them grabbed his hand. I had no time to think. I jumped up, barked, and lunged. Startled, the men took a few steps back. The cabinet started to rock back and forth, making an awful noise. While Claude took hold of the cabinet to stabilize it, the men left the office in a hurry."

I looked at him, hoping to receive a little praise. Instead, he told me that we were in trouble.

"But Tommy," I said, "The men didn't confront and grab me. They shook hands with me. Shaking hands is a custom of friendship. They were supposed to be there. One of them was my landlord. He had made an appointment to show my office to prospective tenants, accountants who were thinking of renting space next door, and wanted to see the layout of my office."

"That's my point," said Tommy. "You knew they meant no harm. They knew they meant no harm. But I didn't know they meant no harm. So, I acted."

Sometimes, we become so adamant about imposing ourselves on a friend that we belabor a point. A casual conversation becomes a heated argument. Emotions rise, and feelings are hurt. Soon, insults will be exchanged. Winning an argument is never worth hurting a friend.

"On second thought," I said. "I think you're right."

Andy turned to Bobby, and said, "I can see that one night, your bravery will repel an attack from two hoodlums, and no doubt about it, they will be genuine foes."

"You and Claude will be walking on a street, and come to a bridge made of concrete blocks. It will be bounded by two narrow sidewalks, one on each side."

"You'll need to cross the bridge to go home, but shuffling past other pedestrians on the sidewalk will be difficult. When the sidewalk is clear from end to end, you'll start your walk. At about the midway point, Claude will notice two men walking toward you. Young and disheveled, they'll keep their heads and hands hidden inside hooded sweatshirts."

"When these no-good hoodlums are close, Claude will hold you against the railing, and ask them to pass you. But they'll stop. Puzzled, Claude will motion for them to keep moving, but they'll just give him a nasty glare."

"Claude will recall a news item about two men on the same bridge accosting a third man and trying to throw him over the railing. Fortunately, two officers in a patrol car intervened in time."

"Sensing trouble, you'll growl, but the men will snicker. Then, you'll lunge at them, but Claude will hold you back. Frustrated, you'll nip Claude's leg. Stunned, the two men will look at each other."

"'Did you see that?' one will ask."

"I sure did. The dog just bit the old man."

They'll laugh, and take turns barking at you, hoping to see you bite Claude again. You'll keep barking and lunging at them, each time more aggressively.

"Eventually, common sense will prevail. They'll realize that if you're capable of nipping your owner in the leg, you're also capable of mauling his enemies. They'll reconsider, and walk away, in search of easier prey."

# Chapter 29

Andy, the dogs, and I were still standing next to the boulder when Andy said, "Who wants to race me down the slope?"
"You should go home," I replied.

"Not yet, we still have time. Just one race around the trees."

We walked to the other end of the park and stopped at the top of the slope. The snow was melting. The ground was wet, but firm.

"Claude, stand over there. I'll stand right here. Both of us have to run down the slope and weave around the trees we meet. The first one who touches the wall of the arena wins the race. Start on the count of three. Are you ready? One… two…" Andy darted down the slope. As he rounded the first tree, he yelled, "three." I started to run.

I was trailing Andy down the slope. He had a good lead, so I improvised. Instead of going around the trees, I started running through them. I passed Andy, touched the side of the arena first, and celebrated my victory.

I noticed for the first time that Bobby and I were both a little winded.

"Not fair," protested Andy. "You ran through the trees, not around them."

"I know. But you started at the count of two, not three." We looked back and saw Tommy limping toward us. "Poor Tommy," I said. "You must be in so much pain." Tommy shook his head.

Andy grabbed a few stones from the ground, and said, "Watch me." He looked around to see if anyone was looking, then threw a stone on the curved roof of the arena. It skipped up and down the roof, making a loud noise, then fell over the edge. He threw two more stones on the roof.

Bobby turned to Andy, and said, "The noise that the stones make on the roof reminds me of the noise that your fingers make on the piano."

Andy chuckled, and said, "Inside the arena, the noise is even louder."

"Suddenly, a man opened the back door of the arena and shook his fist at us. Andy threw another stone on the roof. Infuriated, the man ran after Andy, who dropped the stones and fled around the corner of the arena, Bobby and I kept up with him, but Tommy lagged. We ran alongside the railroad tracks. There were freight cars parked on the tracks, all of them empty, possibly being readied for a load of cattle. We snuck under one of the wagons, and hid behind a set of wheels."

"We shouldn't be here," I told Andy. "Freight cars can move without warning. The wheels can crush us."

Andy shrugged his shoulders, as he peeked around the wheels.

There was a pause, then I asked Andy, "Where is Dad taking you this weekend?" "North Bay."

I nearly choked. "Did you say North Bay?"

My heart started to pound, and my eyes filled with tears.

Startled, Andy said, "Yes. We'll be spending the weekend in North Bay. What's wrong?"

"Is today November 16?" I asked.

"Yes."

"1962?"

"Yes."

"Oh no, oh no. You and John are going to North Bay with Mom and Dad, right?"

Andy nodded.

"But Luc and Pierre are staying at the farmhouse?"

Andy nodded again. Suddenly, his face contorted with dread, and he shouted, "I can see it! Luc will drown today!"

We came out of hiding and ran alongside the wagons. There was a convenience store nearby. I entered the store and saw a stack of newspapers on the counter. At the top of the front page, I read the date: Friday, November 16, 1962. Dazed, I left the store and met the others outside the door. "Indeed, this is the day that Luc will drown."

Tommy shut his eyes, and said, "Now, I know why we're revisiting your past. It's to change your past by saving Luc's life."

"Of course," I said. "I've been alive for a long time. We could be reliving any other day of my past. If we're reliving this one, the worst day in my family's history, and not any other day, there is a reason: to stop Luc from drowning at the farmhouse."

"But how can we save his life?" asked Bobby. "Nobody in this bloody town knows we exist. Nobody can see or hear us."

"Nobody," said Andy, "except me. I can save Luc's life. I have to convince Mom and Dad somehow. I'll tell them as soon as I see them at the house. I'll beg them to take Luc and Pierre with us to North Bay, or else leave John and me behind at the farmhouse." We ran to Andy's house.

His father met him at the door. Furious, he asked, "Where have you been? We should be halfway to North Bay by now. Everybody is waiting for you in the car."

"But I have something important to tell you, Dad!"

"I'm in no mood to listen. Just get in the car."

"But you don't understand…"

"I said get in the car."

"Luc will drown today…"

"In the car, now!"

The car was parked in the driveway. Andy's mother was sitting in the front seat. John was sitting in the back seat with Pierre on his lap. Next to John, Luc was jumping up and down in the back seat. There were no seatbelts. As soon as Andy got inside the car, he sat Luc on his lap. His father put the car in gear and drove down the street. The dogs and I watched the car until it disappeared.

"Do you think that Andy's father will listen?" asked Tommy.

"We won't know if we stay here," I said. "We have to go to the farmhouse." Bobby and I started to run, but after taking a few steps, Tommy winced and hobbled to a patch of grass beside the street. Then, he flopped down.

"Keep going," he shouted. "I need a short rest. I'll be right behind you."

Reluctantly, Bobby and I started to run as the crow flew, through houses, cars, trees, and anything else that stood in our way. When we passed the city limits, I noticed that we were slowing down. I stopped to catch my breath. “Keep running,” insisted Bobby. “We can’t stop now.”

An ambulance raced past us, its siren blaring. Filled with a sense of foreboding, I imagined it responding to an emergency at the farmhouse.

“Run,” urged Bobby.

“I hope we’re not too late. I can hardly breathe. We’re almost there.” I could feel my heart pounding in my chest.

We alternated between running and walking the rest of the way. Finally, I stopped at a driveway longed with trees. Bent over, and taking deep breaths, I said, “This is it. The farmhouse is up the hill, and behind the trees.”

“Look!” exclaimed Bobby, “There is a car coming down the driveway. Isn’t that your family’s car?” I looked up.

The car moved slowly and came to a stop at the end of the driveway. Andy’s parents were sitting in the front seat. Pierre was sitting on John’s lap at the far end of the rear seat. Luc was sitting on Andy’s lap at the near end.

Andy recognized us. Grinning from ear to ear, he rolled down his window, held Luc up to us, and asked, “Where is Tommy?”

I replied, “He’s behind us. He’ll be here soon.”

“I have a favor to ask. Please tell him that I did a great thing today.”

“You did do a great thing. The greatest of things.”

“Make sure Tommy knows.”

“Of course, Andy. We’ll tell him when we see him.”

Andy rolled up the window and hugged Luc. The car turned into the road.

A wave of relief rushed through me. “Luc is safe!” I cheered.

Andy had done it. He had managed to convince Mom and Dad to take Luc and Pierre to North Bay.

Bobby and I hugged.

There was a pause. “Because of Andy, Luc will be able to enjoy a full life. What will he become? When will he marry? How many kids will he have? How long will he live?”

Our elation was intense but short-lived.

# Chapter 30

A fog settled over the landscape. One by one, the trees, the fields, the roads, the cars, everything around us disappeared.

Suddenly, I had a panicky feeling. "Bobby," I gasped. "Tommy is all alone on the side of the road. We must find him before this fog blinds us completely."

"We'll find him," said Bobby, as he began to backtrack. "Follow me."

The fog grew heavier, and the visibility grew poorer. My heart was pounding, and my legs were throbbing. The harder I pushed myself, the weaker I became. Again and again, I stopped to rest.

Bobby was also struggling.

"What's going on?" asked Bobby. "We're losing our strength and our stamina."

Bobby and I retraced our steps. He barked, and I called Tommy's name. Our calls went unanswered, until finally, we heard a high-pitched bark in the distance. "That's him," I said.

"Tommy," I yelled. "We can hear you. We're coming to get you. Keep barking."

Bobby and I walked as fast as possible, guided by the barks, until at last, we found Tommy on the side of the road, close to where we had left him. He was hunched over, and his head was drooping. "There you are," I said. "We found you. What a relief. Guess what? Luc is alive. Andy saved him. He convinced his parents to take Luc and Pierre to North Bay." Tommy smiled.

"Andy was sitting in the car, and Luc was sitting on his lap. We saw Luc with our own eyes. Andy asked us to give you a message. He said, 'Tell Tommy that I did a great thing today.'"

Tommy sighed. His reaction was more subdued than I had hoped.

"In different circumstances," he said, "I would be thrilled."

"What circumstances?" I asked.

There was a pause. He seemed to be searching for his words. Finally, he said, "There's no easy way to say this, so I'll just say it. I'm afraid that we're not revisiting your boyhood town on the eve of a family tragedy."

"Of course we are. We must be."

Tommy shook his head, and said, "I wish I were wrong."

"Where are we then?"

"We're stuck inside a dream."

I looked away in disbelief, and said, "A dream? Why do you think a dream?"

"I'm sure you'll agree that we're not present in this town. We affect nothing in the town, and nothing in the town affects us. When Andy fell down the willow tree, he slipped through your fingers. When we entered the house, we walked through the front door. When you ran down the slope, you ran through the trees. And tell me, who saved Luc? It was Andy."

"We're not visible to anyone. We might as well be sitting alone in a movie theatre, watching a dream unfold instead of a movie."

"But whose dream, Tommy?"

"Yours. This is your town, your park, your house, and your family. This must be your dream. But the dream is coming to an end. I know because the pain is returning to me. I felt it in my leg when we went down the stairs in your house; when we went for a walk around town; and when we ran down the slope. Barely perceptible at first, it intensified over the course of the day, and now, it's become unbearable. The pain is as intense as it was back home, where it robbed me of my mobility and my health."

"I noticed that you were getting weaker. Why not tell Bobby and me sooner? Why did you keep it to yourself?"

"What could you have done? Nothing. I kept quiet because I was enjoying our time together. This dream is unique and instructive. We learned so much about each other. Had I said anything about my pain, we would have talked about the pain, and nothing else."

"Bobby and I learned how we were adopted. We also met your family, and learned about your activities with them: taking midnight swims in the pool; visiting the doughnut shop on walks; and performing at an unfortunate piano recital."

"I learned about your misdeeds: disobeying your parents by climbing up the willow tree; memorizing your prayers in Latin to be reinstated as an altar boy; memorizing a play to atone for smashing a window at school; losing control of your car on the highway; altering your report card; throwing snowballs at cars; teaching Michel how to curse; losing Julie at the fairground; and inciting Richard to skate too fast."

"But I also learned about one good deed: giving the drunken guest directions to the police station, instead of the beer store."

"We reviewed Bobby's misdeeds: taking a mud bath in the public park; stealing your mother's spaghetti leftovers; stealing your pizza slice; picking a fight with the King German Shepherd dog; biting the jogger's shirt in the park; and conducting a cacophony of dog barks in the middle of the night."

"But of course, we also reviewed his acts of courage, sometimes misplaced, and his swimming prowess."

Tommy and I chuckled, then I said, "Tommy, we reviewed your own misdeeds: running away at the ski hill on the coldest night of the year; dragging me on rollerblade skates down the street; pulling me in every direction at the shopping mall; attacking guests at the office; dragging me on my stomach along the icy trail in the forest; and terrifying a horse in its own showjumping ring."

"But we also reviewed your good deeds: playing tag with the cat; playing tag with the rabbit; and enduring the excruciating pain of Lexie's teeth in your ear without retaliating."

"Best of all," I concluded, "we reviewed examples of the protection we gave each other: Bobby shielding me from the hoodlums on the bridge; you preventing the poodle from biting me; you reclaiming for Bobby the bone that the mutt had stolen from him; and me shielding you from the angry homeowner while you squatted on his lawn."

We lost ourselves in a brief reverie, then Tommy spoke again. "The dream is coming to an end. Soon, you'll be fully awake, and I'll be fully paralyzed. In the time I have left, I want to communicate my last wish to you, and I insist that you grant it."

"Before I forget, let me say that I had a wonderful life. You were a good master. You gave me shelter; you gave me food and water; you gave me affection; and you exercised me. Our daily walks were the highlight of my day. You sang to me, and you let me explore my sights and scents. You made me feel loved."

Tommy winced, shifted his weight, and added, "My mobility will never improve. My health will never return. My pain will never cease. Even my appetite is gone forever. The time has come for me to leave this world. The time has come for you to give me a peaceful death."

"I'm not afraid to die. I'm about to enter paradise. I'll be happy there, and I'll be happier when you and Bobby join me. Until recently, I was afraid that death would separate us. But now, I know that death will reunite us in paradise, one by one and that our reunion will last forever. The separation we must each face in this world will be our last."

"Promise me that you'll honor my wish. Make an appointment with the animal clinic first thing."

"And one more point. When I'm lying down at the clinic, waiting to die, and drawing my last breath, be there. Stay with me; brush my hair; hug me; talk to me; sing to me until I'm gone."

"I promise," I said, tears rolling down my cheeks. I hugged him and nodded.

"In a few minutes, you'll be awake. You'll realize that this was a dream. You'll want to believe that it was just a fleeting nightmare. But understand that my wish is real, binding, and irrevocable."

"When you wake up, look at me. I'll confirm my last wish by blinking at you three times. So, look at me."

"I won't let you down."

How ironic. In real life, Tommy was paralyzed, and on the verge of death. He had the most to gain by remaining in the new world, whether it was paradise, my boyhood town, or even a dream. He had the most to lose by returning to his old world and reverting to his old, ailing, and disabled self. Yet, he was the one who had figured out that his transformation had only been a brief respite from his miserable existence.

Fortunately, Tommy was leaving with the conviction that, sooner or later, we would all be reunited forever in paradise.

# Chapter 31

"What a nightmare," I said, waking up. "Am I glad it's over!"

I remembered the symptoms of the night before. I stayed in bed, felt my chest, and took deep breaths. The discomfort was gone. I wondered whether I had suffered a heart attack, or whether my nerves had just flared. I resolved to ask my doctor to run some tests. But first, I had Tommy's last wish to fulfill: "Give me a peaceful death."

I rose from bed and walked aimlessly in the apartment. I knew that Tommy was awake, and staring at me, but I did my best to delay eye contact with him. I showered, got dressed, then went to the kitchen to make breakfast.

Tommy barked. I glanced at him. Before I could look away, he blinked. A few seconds later, I forced myself to look his way. He blinked twice in quick succession.

My eyes welled, and I went into the bathroom to wipe the tears. *Pull yourself together.* I thought. *Tommy needs you now more than ever.*

I went back to the kitchen and fed Bobby. Tommy refused to eat.

I dialed the clinic's number. After informing the receptionist that I had decided to put Tommy down, I asked her how quickly the veterinarians could accommodate me. She replied that they had reserved a slot for me at noon, in case I called. I took it and asked her if we could arrive early, and spend his last hours together. “Of course,” she said. “We’ll be waiting for you.”

I went to my neighbor’s apartment and asked him if he could help me move Tommy to the car again.

“Is it time?” he asked.

I nodded.

He put his hand on my shoulder, then followed me to my apartment. We laid Tommy on a blanket and lifted him gently. Tommy was unresponsive. We carried him to the car and placed him on the floor. My friend whispered something in his ear, then told me, “You’re doing the right thing.” I nodded and drove off.

I’ve often wondered how I would react to Tommy’s passing. In life, I had tried to take care of him. We walked daily. I fed him well. I had a veterinarian conduct regular check-ups. I gave him affection.

But would I be able to do the right thing when it was time to let him go? How would I know when he was too old, his health was too frail, and his suffering was too great? Would my decision to euthanize him be too hasty, and rob him of precious time, or would it be too late, and prolong his misery? And how could I ensure that his passing would be comfortable, or at least tolerable?

I had long ago decided to spend his terminal moments with him. If I had the power to decide when he died, I also had the duty to be with him when he died. I imagined him being alone at the clinic, lying on a gurney as strangers in lab coats and sad faces rushed past him. No, I had to be there and fulfill his last wish.

Would I be able to sing to him? Or would I forget the lyrics of the songs, start crying in midstream, or leave the room in a panic, intensifying his anxiety? It was one thing to sing on a routine walk, and quite another to sing at the end of his life, an end that I myself would be precipitating.

When I parked the car at the clinic, a technician wrapped a blanket around Tommy, carried him to a back room, and placed him gently on a comforter on the floor. Tommy was lying on his side. The assistant asked if I needed anything. I shook my head, and she left the room. I sat behind Tommy and brushed the side of his body. He was breathing slowly. Suddenly, he started to pant. I whispered his name to remind him that I was still there. He sighed. I continued to pet him. My arm grew tired. I laid on my back, rested my elbow on the floor, and started to brush him with my fingers as if my arm were a windshield wiper on a car. I had learned this trick in childhood when giving my father backrubs. If I rested my elbow on a surface, my arm never got tired.

Hoping to make him feel more comfortable, I sang 'Space Oddity' and 'Danny Boy', over and over. I felt the urge to cry but sang through my tears. Tommy began to fidget. He kicked his legs along the surface of the comforter. He wanted to sit upright. I lifted him, but he fell on his side. I lifted him again and placed a pillow under his side. He was able to stay upright and look around him.

In his final months at home, Tommy had spent many of his waking hours sitting on the floor, looking around him. To me, he seemed alert and curious, but to the man who cleaned my apartment every fortnight, he seemed disoriented. I wondered whether I had made Tommy linger too long.

My brother Pierre called me on my mobile phone. I told him that Tommy would be euthanized at noon. "I'm with Richard," he said. "We're coming right now. We'll be there in half an hour. Wait for us."

When they arrived at the clinic, they were ushered to the back room. We took turns whispering to Tommy. A few minutes later, the veterinarian entered the room and asked me if she could proceed. I nodded. She also asked whether I preferred to leave Tommy on the floor or move him to a table. "Let's leave him on the floor," I replied.

She explained that there would be two stages. First, she would give him a sedative to calm him down. A few minutes later, she would give him a barbiturate to stop his heart. She warned us that Tommy's limbs might twitch.

She pricked his hind leg and injected the sedative. Then, she left the room. Pierre brushed Tommy's side and said he could feel the sedative working. Tommy's breathing was shallow. I sang 'Danny Boy' one last time. The veterinarian returned and administered the barbiturate. I hid my face in his mane, hugged him gently, and continued singing. A few minutes later, she interrupted me and pressed the stethoscope against his chest. I stood up, took a deep breath, and put my glasses on the table, waiting for the inevitable announcement.

"Tommy's gone," she said.

I dropped to my knees and sobbed uncontrollably. I sank my head in his mane again, rubbed my face in his thick hair, wrapped my arms around his torso, and squeezed it affectionately. Having clasped my fingers under his belly for months to help him walk, I knew the feeling too well. I apologized to everyone in the room for being so distraught. The veterinarian assured me that all the patrons had left the clinic. "Let it all out," said Pierre. Every time I tried to stop, I felt a new wave of grief rush through me. I went to the washroom and blew my nose.

When I came back, I walked around Tommy, observing him from different angles. His eyes were still open. He looked comfortable. "It was a peaceful death," I said. I hugged Richard. I hugged Pierre. I even hugged the veterinarian and thanked her. She left the room for a few minutes and returned with two pamphlets, one containing advice on how to grieve, and the other outlining options on how to dispose of his remains. I asked what she would do next. She said that she would send the body for cremation. The ashes would be delivered to the clinic in the following week. She would call me then. In the meantime, she invited me to contact her anytime I needed her.

I offered to pay. She declined and suggested that payment be made when I claimed the ashes. I thanked her again for taking such good care of Tommy over the years. Then, Pierre, Richard, and I left the clinic and went to Pierre's house. He poured me a glass of wine, and we reminisced about Tommy. I made a few phone calls to advise my friends.

The wine dulled my guilt, at least temporarily. I had often expressed the hope that, when Tommy died, I would feel grief, but not guilt. I felt the grief right away. As the day progressed, the guilt started creeping up on me. By the next morning, I was racked with guilt. Not about the